Pretty Young Things

2

D1520198

Chase Moore

www.jadedpublications.com

1

"That ain't Starr's car," Antoine said to himself.

He tried to peer into the car through the dark tinted windshield but was only able to see a silhouette. Antoine became irritated and uncomfortable all at the same time.

What the hell is going on?

The red Dodge Charger came to a slow stop, but the engine remained running as the driver gradually stepped out the car.

Antoine stood outside directly in front of his car as he waited for Starr to get out.

Seconds later, Starr's girlfriend Stevie emerged from the vehicle while aiming her gun towards Antoine. Before he was able to recognize what the hell was going on, Stevie quickly pulled the trigger.

POP!

A single bullet instantly tore through Antoine's chest directly beneath his right collar bone. He stumbled backwards upon the impact of the gunshot and fell against the hood of his car. His eyes widened in disbelief as he looked from Stevie down to the dime-sized hole in his chest oozing blood.

Stevie slowly made her way over towards Antoine. Gravel crunched beneath the soles of her sneakers. "Nigga, I hope the pussy was worth it," she sneered.

Jealousy, anger, and the fact that she'd been betrayed by the one person she truly loved had caused Stevie to react impulsively.

Antoine's breathing became harsh as he slowly felt his life slipping away from his body. It was then that his entire livelihood flashed before his very eyes.

He coughed up a mouthful of thick dark red blood as he slid down onto the ground, his knees buckling beneath his weight.

What a messed up way to go out, he thought to himself.

Stevie raised the barrel of the gun to Antoine's head. "You fucked the wrong bitch, bruh..."

Antoine's gaze shifted from the gun to Stevie's cold, dark eyes. "I ain't fuck the wrong bitch," he forced out, wiping the trail of blood off his chin. "I fell for the right one..."

Silence.

Stevie's usually steady hand began to tremble upon hearing his words. Her nostrils flared in anger, and she yearned for nothing more than to blow the nigga's fucking head off.

Her heart shaped lips curled upward as she glared at Antoine. Hatred coursed through her veins, but in her heart she felt a completely different sentiment.

Antoine sat pathetically on the ground, clutching his chest as he continued to stare at the gun. He expected it to go off at any moment...however it didn't.

Stevie slowly lowered her weapon.

Backing away from Antoine while still facing him, she made her way back towards her car. Without saying a word, she climbed into the Charger and skirted off, sparing Antoine's life.

***

Two months later, Diamond sat on her sore ass as she waited for Richard "Rich" Keys' verdict.

Her fingers twitched, and her entire body trembled as she sat on the edge of Rich's California king size bed.

Suddenly, Rich emerged from the steamy master bathroom with a terry cloth towel wrapped around his waist. He had to wash the shit and blood off his dick, but he knew without a doubt that his point had been proven.

Diamond's dry lips trembled as she continued to stare at the carpet. She was totally out of it.

What the fuck has my life become, she asked herself.

Rich didn't bother looking in Diamond's direction as he walked over towards his dresser and pulled out a pair of Hanes Boxers.

"What are you gonna do to me now?" Diamond whispered, barely audible. Her eyes were still glued to the carpet as she spoke. She was literally scared shitless.

Rich turned and faced Diamond after pulling up his boxers. "What?" he asked in a nasty tone. "Come again?"

Diamond slowly looked up at Rich with red-rimmed, tear-filled eyes. There was an 'off' look about her. She definitely didn't look like herself. "I said," she began in a slightly louder tone. "What are you gonna do to me now?" She prayed he didn't respond with '*kill you*'.

Rich proceeded to pull on a pair of True Religions. "I don't know what the fuck I'ma do with ya ass," he said nonchalantly, not looking at her. "I'm still thinkin' about it. Maybe I'll go for a round two tonight...," he teased in regards to the brutal way he'd anally raped Diamond only moments ago.

Just the thought of Rich penetrating her swollen ass again had Diamond feeling squeamish. She couldn't take any more punishment...not to that vicious degree.

"Please, no...," Diamond quickly said.

"Please, no what Diamond?" Rich asked. "Please, no what?" He turned to face her. "I kill mufuckas for the shit you did to me earlier—"

"What if," Diamond paused and looked at the floor.

"What if what?!" Rich barked.

Diamond's eyes slowly lifted as she met Rich's intense gaze. "What if I told you I know who killed your brother...?"

At first Rich believed his ears were deceiving him. "Come again?" he asked.

"I said what if I told you I know who killed—"

Diamond's sentence was instantly cut short after Rich charged her and wrapped a large hand around her slender throat.

"Bitch, what the fuck you just say?!" he sneered.

Diamond tried to pull his hand from around her neck, but Rich was far too strong. Her eyes bulged in their sockets, and her mouth fell open as she made croaking noises.

"Fuck you mean you know who killed my mothafuckin' brother?!" Rich yelled, crushing Diamond's windpipes.

Her eyes rolled to the back of her head as she slowly felt herself nearing unconsciousness.

2

Realizing that he wouldn't get an answer out of Diamond if he killed her, Rich gradually loosened his grip around her throat.

Diamond greedily sucked air into her lungs. After recovering from a brief coughing fit, she finally spoke. "I didn't have...anything to do with shit...I swear," she said in a distorted voice, still struggling to catch her breath.

"Bitch, quit stallin' and tell me what the fuck I need to know!" Rich barked.

"Stevie!" Diamond bellowed.

Rich looked confused. That was the last thing he expected to hear. "Stevie?" he repeated skeptically. "Fuck you mean, Stevie?"

Stevie was one of his most trusted and loyal business associates. He fucked with her heavy, and Diamond's accusation just didn't add up. Or maybe they did and he just refused to believe it.

"Stevie, killed your brother—"

"You better be willing to put that shit on ya mothafuckin' life," Rich warned her.

"I swear!" Diamond promised. "She and her girlfriend Starr set the nigga up and killed him."

Rich rubbed his goatee as he scrutinized the suspicious female in front of him. Less than two hours ago he'd caught her red-handed trying to rob him. "How the fuck you know all this shit?" he demanded to know.

Diamond wiped away her oncoming tears and sniffled. She completely tossed her loyalty out the window when she said, "Starr told me the whole story."

***

"Girl, you should've seen my mothafuckin' face though," Cymphanie Coleman laughed. "The last thing I expected was for the motherfucker *not* to be circumcised." She took an aggressive pull on the blunt and handed it to her younger cousin Starr.

"I'm sure that shit ain't stop you though. Did it?" Starr giggled.

Cymphanie released half of the smoke through her nostrils and the rest through slightly parted lips. "Hell no," she answered. "Girl, I got to peelin' that nigga's dick back like a banana."

Starr burst into a hysterical fit of laughter, accidentally releasing the smoke she held too early. She went into a brief coughing fit and handed the blunt back to her cousin. "Bitch, I cannot deal," she laughed.

"I mean the nigga was fine as fuck, Starr," Cymphanie bragged. "Don't get me wrong. I was just disappointed when I saw that his dick wasn't circumcised." She took a quick pull on the blunt. "The nigga's dick looked like a mothafuckin' body bag," Cymphanie joked. "Ole' crime scene ass dick."

Starr fell backwards on Cymphanie's bed as she howled with laughter.

Cymphanie was Starr's favorite cousin on her father's side of the family. As teenagers, the two used to be extremely close, but after Starr dropped out of high school and began running the streets with Stevie and Diamond, they somehow lost contact.

Cymphanie was the first person, Starr had contacted after she fled Cleveland. Her cousin lived in a beautiful home in Columbus, Ohio and happily welcomed her distraught relative with open arms.

Cymphanie was only two years older than Starr at twenty-five, and her bold attitude is what drew most people to her. She pretty much said whatever was on her mind, and never gave two fucks about how anyone felt after it was said. Either you loved her or you despised her.

Cymphanie didn't work a normal nine to five. Much like Starr's ex best friend Diamond, Cymphanie *claimed* that she was pampered and spoiled rotten by her many 'cake daddies' as she referred to them. She bragged that the men did everything from paying the car note for her BMW 3 series she was pushing to treating her to luxurious trips to foreign countries like Paris, Rome, and Italy.

Cymphanie swore up and down that she didn't want for anything. She was young, wild, and beautiful. Starr could clearly see why the men adored her the way they did. With smooth, blemish-free dark skin, wide doe shaped eyes complemented by long eyelashes, and a pair of full lips, Cymphanie was guaranteed to make heads turn. She had the body of a video model with a small petite waist, thick thighs, and a massive ass that almost seemed too big for her frame. Cymphanie always wore her jet-black hair in a pixie cut which only added to her exotic beauty.

"Anyway, Devon—that's his name, Devon—wants me to be his *exclusively*," Cymphanie continued. "Said he wants me to stop whatever I might have goin' on with any other dude, and if I do that he'll give me whatever I want."

Starr sat up on her elbows and stared admirably at her cousin. "So what you gon' do?" she asked. "What do you want?"

"Bitch, what you mean? I *got* everything I want," Cymphanie laughed. She made her life seem to perfect and stress-free, but if Starr knew the real deal she wouldn't be so impressed.

Starr sighed as she stared off into space with a faraway look in her eyes. She wished she could say she had everything she wanted. In all actuality, she had nothing but a few hundreds left over from the money she and Stevie had worked hard to save over the years. Besides, Cymphanie Starr had no one.

The one person that she thought she couldn't live without had betrayed her in the worst way imaginable.

The day was still fresh in Starr's mind when Stevie confessed to cheating with Diamond. It felt like she'd been stabbed directly in the heart. She'd never felt so much hurt or pain in her entire life.

"I wish I knew what that felt like...," Starr admitted. "This chick right here ain't got shit. I swear Cymph, if it wasn't for you taking me in I don't know what the hell I would've done. I'm so damn grateful, but I really need to get on my feet and get my own shit. Ain't nothin' like having your own. You feel me?"

Cymphanie reached over the edge of her bed and mashed the filter into the plastic ashtray sitting on the carpet. "Girl, I tried to put you on what I was doing years ago, but obviously, you'd rather suck on some pussy than get this paper," she said. "Shit, I'm getting money, and all a bitch gotta do is look pretty." Cymphanie turned to face Starr. "You could get money too if you'd listen to me and let me put you on to some game."

***

ASAP Rocky's *"Max Julien"* blared through the speakers of Rich's black 2012 Lexus ES 350. He was smoking on some of the best loud Cleveland had to offer in order to calm his nerves. Rich's mind was all over the place, and it took everything in him not to choke out the bitch sitting in his passenger seat.

Diamond remained silent as she stared at the passing scenery. Although Rich hadn't said a word since they'd climbed into his car she could clearly feel the tension between them. Diamond didn't know if he was more upset about her trying to rob him or if he was angry about the fact that she'd known all along who killed his brother.

"Where are we going?" Diamond finally worked up enough courage to ask.

Rich turned the music down. "What?" He asked, keeping his eyes on the road.

"Where're we going?" Diamond repeated.

At one point in time she actually dug Rich and his boss-like swag, but after tonight he had her shook. She was undoubtedly afraid of him and what he was capable of. Starr had warned her about him, and Diamond was too foolish to take heed to her friend's warning.

"You swore up and down this bitch Stevie killed my brother," Rich began. "So we finna go find this hoe and get to the bottom of this shit."

"*We*?!" Diamond wasn't feeling that shit. She wasn't feeling it at all. "Why do I have to be with you when you confront her?" she asked. Diamond didn't want to be put in the middle. "You don't believe me or something? You think I'm lying?"

Rich tore his gaze away from the road long enough to look at Diamond. "I hope for *your* sake you ain't," he warned her. "'Cuz if you spin me, I'ma fuck you up Diamond. On everything I love. You thought that lil' shit I did to you earlier was somethin', you ain't seen shit yet," Rich told her. "When I'm done with your ass, you gon' be beggin' for a nigga to kill you. You hear me?"

An uncomfortable feeling settled in the pit of Diamond's stomach upon hearing Rich's threat. "Why're you doing me like this?" she asked in a low tone. "I thought you had feelings for me. I thought you cared about me..."

"I thought the same about you, but you showed me just who you really were," Rich said. "You ain't give a fuck about me, so I'ma show ya ass I can give two fucks about you."

There was a brief pause between the two.

"I'm still the same chick you fell for, Rich," Diamond whispered. She was trying her best to manipulate his mind. "I'm still the same chick you visited in the hospital every day after the accident. Remember that?" she asked. "I'm still her."

Rich didn't respond immediately. For a split second he actually allowed Diamond to get in his head and heart until he suddenly remembered that she'd tried to play him.

If only he'd stuck with his initial plan, he wouldn't be in the situation he was in or feeling the way he did. Rich needed Diamond because she had something beneficial to him. A connect. Somehow he'd gotten feelings for her which slowly developed over time.

Since his lengthy stint in prison, his connect had stopped fucking with him. No connect could trust a person after doing time due to the fact that the person could still be hot or maybe have even snitched. Needless to say, Rich needed a new drug connect, especially since the gun money wasn't enough.

Unfortunately, Rich had quickly lost track of what he needed to do after mixing business with pleasure.

From now on pussy is just that...pussy. You can't trust these hoes. He'd stood firmly by that motto for years—until he met Diamond. "Naw, you ain't," Rich said. "I *thought* you was that chick...but obviously, my judgment was all fucked up—"

"I'm still her, Rich!" Diamond pleaded. "I just made a mistake baby. I'm sorry. Please forgive me."

"Can't do that, Diamond," Rich said nonchalantly.

"You told me you'd take care of me."

"I told you that if you played your *position* I'd take care of you," Rich corrected her. "It was as simple as that. You couldn't even do that shit."

Diamond reached over and lightly touched Rich's arm. "You're mad at me. I understand...but I can make things right. Let's just go home. Let me make it up to you, daddy. Fuck Stevie—"

"The fuck off me!" Rich spat, snatching his arm away from Diamond's treacherous ass. "Like I told ya ass if you playin' with me about this shit, I'ma fuck you up. Plain and simple," he said. "Everything I ever said to you—everything I ever felt about you is long gone now so don't waste ya mothafuckin' time patronizing me. I ain't that nigga. You should know that shit by now. You had a real dude. You fucked that up."

"But Rich—"

"Diamond, I suggest you shut the fuck up before I hit you in ya shit," he threatened.

Diamond quickly complied, fearful that Rich wouldn't hesitate to fold her ass.

Rich took a final pull on his blunt as he neared a yellow light.

It was then that the wheels churned in Diamond's head as she sat silent in the passenger seat. *What if Stevie denies the accusation?* It was Diamond's word against Stevie's, and Diamond had already proved herself to be disloyal and dishonest.

Rich brought the Lexus to a slow stop after the light turned red.

He's probably going to kill me regardless, she told herself.

Immediately, Diamond hit the automatic door unlock button and jumped out Rich's car just as the traffic light turned green. She didn't even bother slamming the door behind her before she took off running!

3

Diamond's heart pounded ferociously in her chest as she ducked and dodged the oncoming traffic. Her ankles wobbled in her six-inch leopard print Lamé Louboutins as she ran across the busy main street. Too afraid to look over her shoulder to see if she was being pursued, Diamond expertly weaved through the traffic.

BEEP!

BEEP!

Drivers honked their horns as they sped around the frantic woman.

All of a sudden, Diamond tripped and crashed against the asphalt, scraping her bare knees. *"Oomph!"*

The moment she looked up she watched as the bumper of a white 2011 Denali rapidly approached her.

SSSSCCCCRRRR!

The tires burned rubber as the driver swerved his truck to the left just seconds before slamming into Diamond. Picking herself up off the ground she took off, leaving one of her shoes behind. She was too shaken up and afraid to go back and retrieve the $1100 heel.

The driver of a 2009 Monte Carlo slowed his car down long enough to get a good look at the panicking woman in the middle of the street.

"Please! Let me in!" Diamond pleaded, banging on the tinted passenger window

Diamond half expected the driver to pull off, but she was surprised when he hit the automatic door unlock button and allowed her access to his vehicle. She wasted no time as she hopped into the stranger's car.

"What's up, ma? Why you runnin' in the street like you crazy or some shit?"

"Please! We have to get away from here! He's going to kill me!" Diamond said. She was behaving hysterically as she looked around to see if she saw Rich's car.

"Damn, what type of shit you in?" the driver asked, pulling off.

Diamond settled into the passenger seat, relieved that she didn't see Rich's car anywhere in sight. "I—uh...I was mugged," she lied. Diamond glanced at the stranger out the corner of her eye to see if he bought it.

He was light brown-skinned with an elongated face, and resembled rapper, Redman.

A Chicago Bulls snapback sat low on top of his head and a toothpick hung out the corner of his thick lips.

"Word? Whatchu' doin' walkin' around alone out here?" he asked. "You too damn pretty to be out here like that, ma."

"I...was...uh—on my way to catch the RTA," she lied, digging herself in a deeper hole.

"You gotta do better, babe. My name is Keesh by the way."

"I'm Diamond...and thanks for picking me up. I really appreciate it."

Keesh switched lanes as he navigated around the slower moving vehicles. "So where you on yo' way to now, Miss Diamond?" he asked, briefly looking over at her.

Diamond watched as he undressed her clothing with his beady eyes. She suddenly felt uncomfortable. She cursed the fact that she was wearing a Michael Kors Stretch wool-crepe dress that revealed her thick shapely legs.

Pulling her dress down, Diamond tried to ignore Keesh eye-fucking her as she searched for her handbag. She knew she couldn't go home, and Starr definitely wasn't coming to her aid so there was only one other person she could think of to call at a time like this.

Where the fuck is my handbag?

"Shit," Diamond cursed, realizing she'd left her handbag—along with her cellphone—inside of Rich's Lexus.

"What's up?" Keesh asked. "Everything cool?"

"I lost my phone," Diamond told him. "Can I use yours? I have to call someone."

"It depends on who you finna call," he told her.

Diamond raised an eyebrow in confusion. "What do you mean?"

Keesh grinned. "Shit, I got you. You in good hands. You ain't gotta call nobody," he said. "Look, I know you had a rough night and shit so check it, I got a bottle at the crib. Why don't you come and chill with me for a minute? Take your mind off all this shit."

Diamond snorted in disgust. "Are you fucking serious?" she asked, her tone dripping with sarcasm.

"Dead ass. Why?"

Diamond shook her head. "Pull over. Let me out the car."

"What the hell is up with you?" Keesh asked, sounding slightly offended.

"You on some other shit, dude. Let me out the car. I ain't in the mood for no extra shit."

Keesh chuckled. "You must be one of those stuck up ass bitches," he said. "You think you too good for a nigga, huh?"

Diamond pulled on the locked door handle. "Did you hear me?! I said let me out the fucking car!"

"What if I don't wanna let you out," Keesh told her. "What if I feel like you might owe me a lil' somethin'—"

"Because you let me in your car?!" Diamond yelled. "Nigga, you got life fucked up! Let me out this—" Her sentence immediately trailed off. Diamond's eyes widened at the sight of the shiny pistol Keesh brandished.

"Okay bitch, I'ma need you to shut the fuck up and ride," he demanded, holding firmly onto the handle of the gun.

Diamond's heart felt like it had dropped into the pit of her stomach as she settled into her seat and reluctantly complied.

Suddenly, Keesh's cellphone rang in his lap. "Excuse me for one second babe," he said sarcastically. "Hello? What's up, Rich? Yeah, I got her ass. She's right here."

Diamond practically fainted at the mere mention of Rich's name. Unbeknownst to poor Diamond, Keesh was one of Rich's right hand men, and much like a bodyguard, he was never too far away just in case some shit popped off. Keesh offered the security that a nigga like Rich couldn't be without when living in a world full of haters and enemies.

"You played me," Diamond said in a bitter tone.

Keesh chuckled. "Nah, baby girl. You played yaself."

"Fuck you and Rich," Diamond said coolly. "How 'bout that?"

Before Keesh could reply, Diamond grabbed the steering wheel!

4

You can keep your hands on me, touch me right there, rock my body...

I can't keep my hands off you. Your body is my party...

I'm doing this little dance for you...

You got me so excited...

Ciara's *"Body Party"* blared through the speakers of Club Twist, an urban gay club located on the west side of Cleveland.

"What's up, girl. Why you actin' like you don't see me though?" Stevie asked, gently grabbing the wrist of a passing brown-skinned female.

Stevie had the waitress send over a complimentary drink, and she hadn't even gotten as much as a thank you. Obviously, the chick was playing hard to get. Either that or she was just flat out rude.

"It's gon' take more than just a lil' ole drink to get my attention," she smiled, revealing the sexiest pair of dimples.

Stevie pulled her closer to her body. "For real?" she bit her bottom lip. "What's it gon' take?"

Stephanie Marie Thompson aka Stevie was a young, light-skinned stud that stood at five feet eight inches tall, and was rather slender in frame. Her pink heart shaped lips were full, the corners pulled upward into a slight smirk. Stevie's dark almond shaped eyes were complemented by long, thick lashes. She was sexy as hell and she knew it.

The female leaned in closer towards Stevie. Her minty breath tickled Stevie's nose. "Real effort," she said before walking off.

Stevie was left speechless.

"Man, fuck that uppity hoe, B," Max said, waving his hand dismissively.

Maxine "Max" Rogers was one of Stevie's closest homies. No one would ever suspect that he was born a female since he looked so much like a man. A few years ago he'd gotten a double mastectomy in order to have his breasts removed. A sex change operation came shortly after, and the area where her vagina used to be was now a misshapen one-inch penis.

Hormones had given Max the appearance and voice of a man, and he couldn't be happier living his new life as a guy...even with a tiny dick.

Stevie shook off the feeling that her pride had been wounded. So accustomed to being in a relationship, she'd easily become rusty in the dating game. "That's why I'm finna start fuckin' with these white girls," she bragged. "These sistahs don't know how to act."

***

Keesh's eyes rolled to the back of his head as he gripped his neck. Gagging noises came from his throat as he struggled to breath, but every time he tried the toothpick he swallowed inched further down his windpipe. The toothpick was positioned horizontally in his throat, and painfully sliced into his trachea.

After Diamond grabbed the steering wheel, the two had managed to veer off the road before slamming into a fire hydrant.

Keesh had slammed face first into the steering wheel, and Diamond bumped her head against the glove compartment. The minor accident didn't slow Diamond down in the least. She was already halfway up the street when people approached the scene to investigate and seek assistance.

Walking up the partially lit street somewhere in the hood with only one shoe on her feet, Diamond had never felt so alone and pathetic. She sniffled and wiped away the fresh blood underneath her nose, smearing it across her coffee brown cheeks.

Diamond looked like a crack head looking for her next fix as she walked alongside a spray painted brick building. Her expensive designer dress was stained with her own blood, her hair was disheveled, and she didn't have so much as a dollar to her name.

"*Fuck!*" she cursed. Tears uncontrollably slipped from her eyes as she trudged up the dark, litter-filled sidewalk.

A group of niggas stood on the corner of the street. Swallowing her pride, Diamond carefully approached them. She quickly wiped her tears away and pulled herself together.

"Do any of you have a cellphone?" she asked timidly.

"Yeah," one of them spoke up.

"Can I use it?"

The group of hood niggas looked Diamond up and down.

"Yeah, but what the fuck you gon' do for me?" he asked.

His boys snickered after the rude comment.

Diamond sighed in frustration. "I don't have any money on me," she admitted.

"What's up with that head then?" he insisted.

His boys immediately burst into a hysterical fit of laughter.

Diamond sucked her teeth, disgusted by his stupid question and walked off. Never was she that desperate to suck some dirty ass dick just to use a cellphone.

"What?" the hoodlum yelled after her. "You too good to suck some dick, bitch?!"

***

Kabal navigated through the crowd of transvestites, undercover brothers, and studs as he briskly made his way towards Stevie. He was a young, scruffy brown-skinned dude with shoulder length dreadlocks that resembled rapper, Cash Out.

Stevie was stationed at the bar, sipping on a Corona and bopping her head to the bass of the music.

Pulling his cellphone out his pocket, he sent a short text message to his boss Rich that read: *I got her. She here.*

"Hey, excuse me. Can I get two seconds of your time?" A tall, slender brown-skinned guy tugged on Kabal's arm.

"Fuck off me, nigga!" Kabal snatched his arm away. "Fuck wrong witchu?" he spat.

The guy held his hands up defensively and backed away. After all, Kabal wasn't there to meet and mingle with the gay community.

Rich had notified every street nigga he was affiliated with to find Stevie, and bring her to him alive. He wouldn't be able to sleep peacefully until he knew the truth. He had goons everywhere in and around the city looking for her.

Stevie skeptically watched as one of Rich's homeboys approached her. *Is he...*she wondered. *Naw. Can't be...Can he?*

When Kabal finally reached Stevie, he noticed her giving him the side eye. "Nah," he chuckled, reading her mind. "It ain't even like that," he told her. "I been lookin' all over the city for you. The nigga Rich wanna see you," he said casually, not wanting to raise her suspicions.

Stevie didn't think anything of it. "Aight." She turned to her homie, Max and dapped him up. "Guess I'm callin' it an early night since the boss needs me."

"Aight. I'll get up with you later," Max promised.

Stevie followed Kabal to the parking lot. "Rich at the spot?" she asked him, referring to the strip club Rich owned. "I'll follow you over there."

"Nah, he actually right up the way," Kabal told her. "You might as well ride with me. I'll bring you right back to your whip afterward," he promised.

Again Stevie didn't think anything of it. Shrugging her shoulders, she followed Kabal to his glossy black 2010 Dodge Challenger and climbed into the passenger seat.

5

"*Aaahh*! Shit!" Diamond cursed in pain after stepping on a piece of broken glass. She lifted her bare foot and looked to see if she was bleeding. She was.

Tears filled Diamond's eyes as she stared up at the dark starry sky. The full moon hid partially behind thin wispy clouds. A swift breeze through her tangled weave.

"Why are you punishing me?" Diamond asked. She'd never been a firm believer of religion, but after tonight she knew that a higher power had to have been punishing her for her decadent, self-indulgent ways. "I'm not perfect—and I know I'm not perfect—but I'm far from being a damn monster. I lived my life the only way I knew how so why are you fucking punishing me?!"

Diamond looked ridiculous talking to the sky with only one shoe on, a bloodied foot, and her clothing and hair disheveled.

Realizing how foolish she looked, Diamond returned back to reality and continued her stroll up the street. She neared a bus stop and spotted an older woman sitting on the bench minding her business.

Limping over towards the bus stop, Diamond prepared to stoop to an all-time low. "Excuse me," she said in her most polite tone. "Do you have a cellphone I could use?"

The older woman frowned at the very sight of Diamond. "No," she answered smugly.

Diamond felt as if the woman was looking down on her, and she hated the way she felt inside. She felt like crap for looking like a strung-out prostitute or some shit.

Diamond licked her dry lips and raked a hand through her untamed mane. "Well, do you at least have some change for me to use the payphone?" she asked.

The older woman sighed in agitation and searched through her oversized purse. Evidently, she found Diamond to be a nuisance. After locating three quarters, she begrudgingly handed the spare change to Diamond careful not to touch her.

"Thank you," Diamond smiled. *Petty bitch.*

Diamond hurriedly limped off in the direction of the nearest payphone where she proceeded to dial up the one and only person she could think to call.

***

Stevie shuffled nervously in the passenger seat as an uncomfortable feeling settled in the pit of her stomach. Her stomach bubbled and she felt a bad case of gas coming on which happened whenever she got nervous.

Stevie couldn't explain it but something felt off. "So...why Rich wanna see me?" she finally asked.

Kabal shrugged a shoulder. "I don't know," he answered. "He ain't tell me why. I'm sure it ain't shit though. Relax."

Stevie could do any and everything *but* that. Her stomach churned and begged for her to release the gas, but she squeezed her ass cheeks together to keep from letting go. "Relax?" she repeated skeptically. "Why would I need to relax if it ain't shit? Obviously, it's important if he got you combing through the whole city to look for me. So I'ma ask you again...what Rich want with me?"

"Look, I told yo' mothafuckin' ass I don't know. So calm down with all that hype shit you spittin'!"

No longer beating around the bush, Stevie boldly snatched out her Glock and placed the barrel of it against Kabal's temple. "Aight, enough bullshittin'," she spat. "Pull this mothafucka over!"

"Bitch is you fuckin' crazy?" Kabal angrily yelled.

"Nigga, did I mothafuckin' stutter?!" Stevie screamed. "Pull this bitch over!"

Kabal huffed and puffed as he brought his Challenger to a slow stop on the side of the street. He shook his head in disbelief as he snatched the gears into park and patiently waited for Stevie to get her ass out his car.

"It's all good," Kabal told her, unfazed by the little tantrum Stevie displayed. "Rich gon' handle that ass for what you did to his brother. Believe that shit."

So the cat's finally out of the bag, Stevie thought to herself. *I knew some funny shit was   up.*
She cocked the Glock. "That's if he ever find's me..."

POP!

Kabal's head dropped limply against his left shoulder after a single bullet tore through his temple. Blood and brain matter painted the driver's window. His eyes were wide open. He didn't even see the shit coming.

Stevie hastily hopped out the car and fled the fatal scene.

***

Diamond's most loyal trick, LaVelle happily came to her rescue the minute she called him to pick her up. He put her up in four-star hotel, and gave her a little spending money all in exchange for some pussy of course.

Diamond felt soulless as she sat positioned on her hands and knees and allowed LaVelle—a married man—to ram into her pussy from behind.

"Damn, baby this shit feels so good!" LaVelle moaned as he slammed his pelvis against her thick ass. "And it smells so fuckin' good. Nice and sweaty just how I like that shit!"

Tears spilled over Diamond's lower lids as she stared straight ahead. She'd died inside after this depressing night.

Ignoring the mental, emotional, and physical pain, Diamond allowed LaVelle to stick his thumb inside her sore asshole while he hit it from the back. Instead of telling him the shit hurt like hell, she resorted to silently crying.

6

The following morning, Starr sat positioned on her knees kneeling over the toilet inside Cymphanie's bathroom. The moment she rolled out of bed she'd suddenly been hit with a bad case of morning sickness.

Holding her hair back, Starr uncontrollably vomited until she was spitting up nothing more than stomach acid. When she finally finished, she wiped her wet mouth with the back of her hand and flushed the toilet.

Scratching her ass, Cymphanie stepped inside the bathroom. "What's up, boo?" she greeted in a muffled voice. Her eyes were partially open and it was evident that she'd just woken up. "I know you ain't in here throwing up."

Starr stayed planted on her knees right in front of the toilet just in case she got sick again. "Yeah, I don't know what's up," she shook her head and lightly rubbed her tummy.

"Well, you ain't pregnant, are you?" Cymphanie asked, padding over towards the sink so she could brush her teeth.

Antoine quickly came to mind, but Starr immediately brushed the thought away. She figured there was no way she could be pregnant by him when they had worn a condom. Unfortunately, Starr had no idea that the condom had broken in the midst of their lovemaking.

"No," she answered. "I can't be pregnant."

Cymphanie chuckled as she squeezed a small portion of Crest toothpaste onto her tooth brush. "Oh yeah. I forgot you can't get pregnant bumping pussies," she teased.

Cymphanie had gay jokes for days, but luckily Starr was used to them.

"Maybe it was something I ate," Starr said dismissively. "I'm sure I'll feel better once I get something on my stomach."

***

That afternoon Cymphanie and Starr strolled through Polaris Fashion Place. A trendy mall located just minutes from downtown Columbus. Both women were shopping for outfits to wear for tonight's fruitful endeavor. Cymphanie was on a mission to teach her little cousin how to effortlessly bag a cake daddy, and the first thing they had to do was purchase some enticing outfits.

Starr tossed her long, wavy hair over her shoulder. She now sported it with a small portion shaved off similar to the singer Cassie's signature hairstyle. "I wanna check out Express," she told her cousin, pulling her in the direction of the popular retail store.

"Cymphanie?" A deep voice called out from behind, stopping both women in their tracks.

Cymphanie turned on her heel to see who had called her name, although she already knew who the familiar voice belonged to.

Standing a few feet away was a handsome tall, dark-skinned guy holding the hand of a toddler. On his right was a pretty, slender, light-skinned female who didn't look very pleased to see Cymphanie.

Cymphanie sighed dramatically and propped a hand on her curvy hip. "What do you want Jason?" she asked.

"*What do I want*?!" he repeated. "You comin' at me like I ain't standin' here with *your* son."

Cymphanie barely took one look at her own child as she glared at her baby's father and his girlfriend.

"Like I said, what do you want?" she asked nonchalantly, popping the gum she was chewing.

Cymphanie gave birth to a beautiful, healthy baby boy two years ago, but one would never know it unless they saw the faint C-section scar on her lower abdomen. A few months after having Jason Jr., she dumped his father and her responsibilities as a parent on him so she could live her life the way she always wanted to.

"When you gon' get your son for the weekend?" Jason asked. "You promised you would weeks ago, and I ain't heard from ya ass since."

"Yeah it'd be nice if Jason and I got a break every once in a while so we could spend some quality time," his girlfriend Jamie chimed in.

Cymphanie was two seconds away from shutting her shit down by telling her that just last month Jason had slid through for some pussy. She wondered how much quality time Jamie would want to spend with him after hearing that.

Cymphanie pointed an accusatory finger at Jason. "Look, nigga, you begged for a damn baby now you got it," she said.

Starr silently stood off to the side as she watched the three of them interact. She couldn't believe the way her cousin was talking and behaving in front of her son. Starr thought the shit was cold, but she decided against speaking on it. After all, the situation didn't have anything to do with her.

Jamie was pissed off at that bit of news. She instantly turned to face Jason. "All this time I been wanting to have a baby, and you begged this bitch to have a child?!" she screamed. "Are you fucking kidding me?!"

Jason started to defend himself but Jamie quickly stomped off, leaving him to feel foolish.

"You foul as hell," he told Cymphanie. "You know that, right? I might've wanted a kid more than you, but that doesn't excuse you from being a mother."

Cymphanie sucked her teeth. "I ain't got time to be nobody's fuckin' mama," she argued. "I'm too busy gettin' money and living life." Cymphanie pointed to Jason Jr. who stood innocently by his father's side, holding onto his leg for support. "You wanted the lil' nigga now you got him. Now I suggest you raise up out my face and go check on ya girl."

Jason shook his head in disgust. "That fucked up attitude of yours gon' be yo' downfall," he warned her. "Just watch." With that said he picked his son up and walked away from his childish ass, selfish baby's mother.

***

The soles of Antoine's gym shoes scraped against the basketball court's maple flooring. Alone in the empty gym, he used his free time to practice his three-point shooting. Since the incident under the bridge, Antoine's shot just hadn't been the same.

The bullet that had impaled his chest had damaged a major vital causing severe nerve damage. Antoine simply couldn't accept the fact that his superior basketball skills was slowly deteriorating before his very eyes.

After the twelfth brick shot bounced off the basketball's rim, Antoine walked off the court, not bothering to fetch the ball. Discouraged and bitter, he'd never felt so depressed in his young life.

Antoine plopped down on the bench and stared off into the distance. *This is some bullshit.* His life and career was over, and it'd only be a matter of time before the team had no choice but to let him go. *What am I going to do then*? He didn't have a backup plan. All he ever wanted to do in life was play ball.

Antoine sighed in frustration and dropped his head into the palm of his hands. He'd never been a vindictive type of dude. He was brought up in a decent two-parent middle class family, and was considered by most as a good person. However, Antoine couldn't help but wonder how nice it'd be to dish out some much deserved revenge.

"Nigga, I hope the pussy was worth it."

Stevie's spiteful words played over and over in his mind. Antoine concluded that it wasn't worth it all. Starr hadn't hit him up since their last encounter, and he had nothing to show for but a bullet wound scar, broken heart, and a fucked up shot.

***

I stay down with my day one niggas, and we in the club screamin' no new friends...

No new friends...

No new friends...

No, no, no new...

DJ Khaled's club anthem "*No New Friends*" bumped through the massive speakers of the popular Columbus strip club, Playpen.

Starr and Cymphanie were the baddest chicks up in the spot and they were only spectators. Starr looked sexy as hell in a studded nude leatherette two-piece Bodycon dress. On her pedicured feet was a pair of beige platform Red Bottoms—the real deal, none of that cheap knock off shit—and her makeup was subtle yet done to perfection.

Cymphanie looked stunning in a Melika purple and black Scuba dress. She was rocking a pair of $1400 black Zoulou Louboutins. Her flawless dark-brown skin seemingly glowed.

Dudes were breaking their necks to get just a second of their attention. Both women were the stars and they weren't even certified celebrities.

Cymphanie had met most of the dudes she fucked with inside of strip clubs. It was the only reason she even frequented gentlemen's clubs. Besides enjoying the unadulterated entertainment, she was always scoping the scene for a nigga that looked worth her time.

Fuck all y'all niggas except my niggas...

One more time...

Fuck all ya'll niggas, except my niggas...

Fuck all ya'll niggas, stay down from day one so I say...

Two tatted up thick redbones were performing pole tricks together on the massive stage in the center of the spacious strip club. Dollar bills littered the stage like rain sprinkling the earth.

Starr suddenly felt someone gently grip her wrist and slowly pull her towards them. "Excuse me, ma," a sultry, deep voice whispered in Starr's ear. "My name Famous, but they call me Fame. So tell me...what a nigga gotta do to spend some quality time with you?"

7

I hope all ya grindin' pay off and turn to dough...

I hope ya niggas never snitch and turn to po'...

I hope ya bitches is faithful and never turn to hoes...

I hope when you roll that shit up and light it its burning slow...

Tatiana aka Luxury danced seductively to Los and Wiz Khalifa's mellow single *"Burn Slow"*. She and Rich were alone in the VIP section of Fantasy's, the popular strip club he owned.

Rich took a puff from the tightly rolled blunt as he watched Tatiana wind her hips to the slow beat of the song. Her moves were hypnotizing as she performed for the one and only man who somehow managed to steal her heart.

Tatiana freed her C-cup breasts and pushed them together before licking her rigid nipples in a rapid, enticing motion.

Rich grabbed his crotch and stroked his hard on as he watched her effortlessly tease him. Using his index finger, he ushered for her to come closer. He licked his lips. "Come over here...sexy mothafucka."

Tatiana slowly danced her way over towards Rich and climbed into his lap.

Just then, Rich's goons walked into the VIP room. They looked like some straight killers dressed in black attire from head to toe, and they'd go to war for Rich if need be. Those were the type of cats that Rich kept in his corner.

"Tell me you got some good news," Rich said.

Tatiana continued to dance seductively in Rich's lap.

"Keesh in the hospital," one of them spoke up. "And they found Kabal's body inside his car."

Rich sighed in irritation and massaged the bridge of his nose. Those were two of his best soldiers. He was fuming inside, but unusually calm on the outside.

"No sign of Stevie either," his goon continued with his arms clasped together in front of him. He prepared himself for an outburst of rage...but it never came.

"I don't give a fuck what you gotta do," Rich said in an even, calm tone. "Find that dyke ass hoe. Tear this mothafuckin' city apart. Do whatever you gotta do, 'cuz a nigga ain't gon' rest 'til this shit's handled. Don't let me down, B."

"Come on, man. I never choke," his goon reassured him. "You got it."

The guys filed out of the VIP room leaving Tatiana alone with Rich and his thoughts.

Rich massaged his temple with one hand, feeling a bad headache approaching.

Tatiana hated to see her boo upset and stressed out. If she could she'd take the weight off his shoulders and put it on her own. That's how much she loved him.

Leaning towards his ear, she whispered, "Don't worry yourself, bay."

Rich released a deep sigh. "Easier said than done..."

"They'll get her. I know they will," Tatiana assured him.

Rich gently cupped her face with his hand and pulled her towards him as if he were preparing to kiss him. He gracefully blew her a shotgun which she eagerly sucked in.

Afterward he pressed his thick lips against hers and slipped his warm, wet tongue inside her mouth. Tatiana savored the aggressive way he took control of the kiss as she melted into his muscular body.

After the tantalizing kiss, Tatiana already knew what time it was. Without deliberation, she dropped between Rich's legs and proceeded to unbutton his True Religions.

Rich reclined his head and closed his eyes. "*Mmm*," he moaned as she slipped his dick in her warm mouth.

Tatiana greedily sucked on his pole like she had something to prove. She figured she could easily replace Diamond, but little did she know she'd never be able to do that. Because as much as Rich hated to admit it he was still in love with Diamond's scandalous ass.

8

3 Weeks Later.

"Hurry up, Diamond. I gotta go pick my kids up from school soon," Orlando complained.

He lay positioned on his back on the cheap carpet of the hotel room. Holding his semi-flaccid penis, he tried to keep it from going completely limp while impatiently waiting for Diamond to do her thing.

Orlando was an attractive light-skinned Al B. Sure looking dude that Diamond messed with from time to time. He never wanted to fuck. Instead he wanted to do every little freaky thing under the sun that didn't involve intercourse. Orlando was married and believed that if he didn't stick his dick in another female, he wasn't necessarily cheating.

Diamond stood directly over Orlando and took another chug from the Deer Park water bottle. "I'm trying," she said, clearly irritated.

Orlando sighed in frustration. "I'm waiting..."

Diamond fondled her belly button a little. "Okay. Here it comes," she said, squatting over Orlando so he could get what he paid for.

Urine splashed onto Orlando's chest, neck, and face. He opened his mouth to catch some of the stream. "Mmm," he moaned in pleasure. "Don't stop."

Diamond's stream lessened until it was nothing more than a few drips. "That's all I got."

Orlando wiped his face with his hand as if he'd just come up from swimming. "I told ya ass to hold ya pee until I got here," he said disappointedly.

"I couldn't," Diamond told him. "When I gotta pee, I gotta pee. I'm not trying to fuck around and get a urinary tract infection messing around with you," she complained.

"Hush all that shit up and get ya ass down here," Orlando said, pulling Diamond down beside him onto the damp carpet. "Open ya legs," he instructed.

Diamond spread her thick thighs apart as far as she could. Silently, she watched as Orlando poured the remaining contents of the water bottle inside her pussy.

Diamond had orchestrated this trick so many times for Orlando. Tightening her pussy muscles, she pushed outward, spraying the contents out.

Orlando's eyes lit up like a kid on Christmas as he watched Diamond squirt water from her pussy. He started drinking the shit like he was sipping from a water fountain. Once there was nothing left to drink up, Orlando proceeded to eat her pussy out as he jacked his dick off. He didn't mind the putrid odor of urine or the fact that they lay in it. He was a freaked out nigga that got off on doing some of the nastiest shit, but he paid good money for Diamond's services so she couldn't really complain. Besides, she needed the money.

After paying for a good time, Orlando rushed out leaving Diamond to scrub the pissy carpet before the smell of urine settled into it and became permanent. Once she finished the disgusting chore, she took a long, hot shower and scrubbed her body until it was raw.

After toweling herself off, she slid into a terry cloth robe and did a quick line of coke to ease her mind. LaVelle had been supplying the old habit she'd recently started doing again. He had some pure, authentic shit too.

Tilting her head back she allowed the coke to run down her throat.

Walking over towards the foggy bathroom mirror, Diamond swiped her hand over it in order to get a good look at her reflection. She immediately regretted it the moment she saw herself.

Dark bags resided beneath her usually wide, vibrant eyes. She hadn't been sleeping well lately.

Diamond ran a hand over her cheek. Her skin was drier than the Sahara Desert. Dozens of heat bumps had made their home on her forehead since she hadn't been taking care of her skin.

Look at yourself.

Look at what you've become over the years.

Suddenly, Diamond burst into hysterical cries. She'd been holding it in since the night she hopped out Rich's car. Her life had quickly spiraled downhill. She felt lower than low.

***

"*Ahh*, shit! Damn, bay," Fame groaned in pain.

"My bad boo," Starr apologized, repositioning herself. She'd accidentally tugged on his catheter.

Fame had been shot in the bladder when he was fourteen years old during a brawl with a rival hood. Sadly, ever since then he was forced to drain his urine through the permanent catheter.

Besides that major flaw, Fame was actually a very handsome dude. Standing at six feet four inches, he was cut up from a daily workout regimen. Fame was dark-skinned, sported a low haircut rippled with waves and a neatly trimmed goatee. He was a pretty boy with hood nigga characteristics. From the neck down, his entire body was covered in tattoos which was a major turn on for Starr.

Fame Jackson produced some of the hottest beats for well-known rappers and singers. He made a pretty penny too, and he never missed an opportunity to spoil Starr rotten.

Fame would have been perfect if he wasn't so possessive and controlling. He clocked all of Starr's moves like an over-protective father and they'd only been kicking it for three weeks.

"You good, bay," Fame assured Starr, palming her tiny firm breasts.

Starr took her time as she rode Fame's lengthy dick like a pro. "Aight. How it feel?" she asked.

Fame met her slow strokes with his own steady ones. "Shit you already know you got that good shit, ma," he admitted. "I don't even know why you gotta ask a nigga."

Starr seductively bit her bottom lip. "I like to hear it," she whispered.

Antoine gave her left ass cheek a firm slap. "You got some good ass pussy, bay."

Hearing Fame say it was like music to her ears. He wasn't Antoine by far—and Starr didn't think it was possible to fall for any other dude but him—but for the time being Fame would have to suffice since he was the next best thing.

Fame had moved Starr out of her cousin's home into a beautiful, newly-constructed townhome in Lancaster, Ohio. Stevie quickly became a thing of the past.

As a matter-of-fact, Starr highly doubted she'd ever fuck with another female. She was having too much fun playing on team dick.

9

Cymphanie held the base of Devon's uncircumcised dick as she sucked on the tip just the way he liked it. She was positioned on her knees while Devon sat on the edge of the bed. It felt as if she were sucking on a bunch of damn skin as she performed oral. However, she decided to keep her thoughts to herself.

"Damn, keep doing it just like that," Devon coached, grabbing a fistful of the bed sheets. His toes curled as he felt a powerful climax approaching. "Here it comes," he breathed heavily.

Seconds later, Devon shot everything he had to offer inside of Cymphanie's oral cavity. She spit the bitter tasting cum all over his glossy dick and rubbed the contents all around his shaft just the way he liked it.

"Yes...you know just how I like that shit," Devon moaned.

Cymphanie proceeded to massage his semi-erect dick. "Daddy, I need a lil' money to get the whip fixed," she lied.

"Well, what's wrong?" Devon asked. "I might be able to take a look at it," he offered.

Damn, nigga. Just give me the fucking money.

"No, babe. Don't worry about it. That's what the mechanics are for. Plus, I don't know exactly what's wrong with it. I gotta get a diagnostic," Cymphanie explained. "So just gimme the money and I'll take care of it."

Devon released a deep sigh. He knew there had to be a price to pay for the awesome head he'd just received. A woman didn't slob a nigga down that good without expecting some shit in return.

"Have you thought any about what we discussed the other day?" Devon asked, grabbing his jeans off the carpet.

"Yeah...but I told you I need time," Cymphanie said smugly.

Devon was still pressing the issue about them being exclusive, but she just wasn't ready. Truth be told, Cymphanie had commitment issues. She loved the freedom to be able to change up whenever she felt herself getting too close to a dude. Life was easier when emotions weren't involved.

"Well, you need to figure out what you gon' do," Devon told her matter-of-factly. "I ain't gon' be waitin' on ya ass forever. It's a lot of bitches out here lookin' for a real nigga."

Yeah, yeah. Whatever. Quit talking my ear off and come up off them bills, Cymphanie thought to herself.

Digging in his jeans pocket, Devon pulled out his leather wallet. After retrieving the small knot of money inside, he peeled a few bills off and handed them to Cymphanie.

"Aight, I'm finna hop in the shower," Devon told her before planting a kiss on her forehead. "Feel free to join me if you'd like," he added.

I think not, Cymphanie said to herself.

She frowned at the chump change he'd just given her. One would have thought she'd asked for money for the Laundromat or some shit.

Devon stood up and headed towards the master bathroom.

Cymphanie made a disgusted face at the sight of the sweat spot left on his bed sheets from where he'd been sitting. She was happy that they weren't at her crib. Cymphanie never allowed her many tricks to know where she lived. She didn't need any drama at the place where she laid her head.

"Nigga, you should know me better than that," Cymphanie mumbled under her breath.

The moment she heard the shower water run, she rummaged inside of Devon's jeans pocket and stole the entire knot of money. Cymphanie didn't just stop there. She ransacked his jewelry chest located on top of his dresser and snatched two rings and a diamond bracelet.

After dressing hastily, Cymphanie fled Devon's home before he realized he'd just been robbed. She fronted with everyone like she was some thoroughbred broad who had all these different niggas caking her when in all actuality, she was a scandalous chick who got off on robbing dudes when they least expected it.

Once Cymphanie made it to a red light at an intersection, she pulled out her cellphone and dialed a familiar number. It'd been so long since she used it, but lately she couldn't seem to get him off her mind no matter how hard she tried or how many men she used to fill the empty void.

The line rang four times before a sexy, deep voice filled the receiver. "Yo."

"Hey, baby," Cymphanie purred.

There was a deep sigh on the opposite end of the line. "Whatchu want, Cymphanie?" he asked, clearly frustrated. "I got a lot of shit on my mind right now."

"I had you on my mind," she told him. "To be honest I always got you on my mind. Don't you ever think about me, bay?"

"Naw...I don't. You're there and I'm here. Plus, I'm too busy tryin' to make shit happen."

Cymphanie's pride felt wounded. "So you mean to tell me that you never think about me?" Tears formed in her eyes.

"Look, I'm busy right now and ain't really got time for this shit—"

"I wanna come back," Cymphanie blurted out. "I thought me coming out here was the right thing to do but, Rich baby, I miss you so much. I can hardly sleep."

Rich sighed in frustration. "Cymphanie...lemme ask you a question, ma," he began. "Are you in school right now?"

Cymphanie's heart dropped into the pit of her stomach. When she stopped dancing at Fantasy's and fucking with Rich, she claimed she was moving to Columbus to attend OSU. She'd done everything under the sun *but* enroll in college including having a son.

Rich wasn't bitter at all about Cymphanie wanting to lead a better life. As a matter of fact, he believed in her pursuing an education and future so much that he shot her a cool ten grand and brought her first whip.

Needless to say, Rich was disappointed when he checked up on her a year later and discovered she wasn't doing shit with her life.

Aside from his hurt feelings, Cymphanie had also cost him precious money.

Since getting caught up with Cymphanie, Rich had promised never to get emotionally involved with another female. He refused to get caught slipping again. No one wanted to feel as if they'd been played, and that's exactly what Cymphanie had done to him.

Rich had stood firmly by his self-made promise all up until he met Diamond. Much like Cymphanie, she had put on a good front in the beginning only to betray him in the end.

Little did these women know, they were the reason behind Rich's doggish ways. They'd transformed him into the very monster that he was to this day.

"No, I'm not in school," Cymphanie answered.

Rich already knew what the answer was before she said it. "Good bye, Cymphanie."

"But—"

Click.

"Hello?" Cymphanie pulled the cellphone away from her ear and stared at it. Rich had hung up right in her face.

***

"It's crazy how hoes be wantin' to come back when shit ain't goin' they way," Rich said. "Anyway back to what we were talking about." He continued to break his weed down.

"Diamond still hasn't been home yet," Rich's hood informant told him. "Honestly, I feel like the bitch is hidin' somethin'. I mean why else would she up and disappear like that?"

Rich licked the tightly rolled blunt closed. "Could be scared."

"Could be..."

Rich chuckled. "I tend to have that effect on bitches," he said. "Either they fear me or they love me..."

10

Pull up in the new 'rarri...

Living like John Gotti...

Choppin' bricks like karate...

Starr rolled over in bed and expected to bump into Fame, but quickly realized that she was alone. Grabbing her cellphone off her nightstand, she subconsciously answered the phone without looking at the caller ID first.

"Hello?" Starr replied in a muffled voice.

"Starr...please don't hang up," Stevie said in a low tone. "I know I'm the last mothafucka you wanna talk to. You probably hate me after the foul shit I did to you—shit, I hate myself. But baby I really need you right now." Stevie sniffled and wiped her nose.

She sat inside her car, parked along the curb of a side street in the hood she grew up in. She couldn't think of anyone else to call during a time like this.

"What do you want?" Starr spat, annoyed with the mere sound of Stevie's voice.

"I'm in some shit right now babe," Stevie admitted. "And I ain't got nobody—no money—nothing."

Starr sucked her teeth. She didn't feel the slightest bit guilty that she had cleaned out the bank account funds that she and Stevie had worked so hard to save up. "You've got friends," Starr said matter-of-factly. "What about Max?"

"I been layin' low over his house for a few weeks, but he ain't able to look out for me no more. Some of Rich's niggas went up to the barbershop he owns and tore the place up. They even roughed Max's ass up lookin' for me, and Max ain't tryin' to be caught in the middle no more," Stevie explained. "He's scared...and to be honest...I am too." She sighed in frustration. "Starr...man...we fucked up. We fucked up bad—"

"What the hell do you mean we fucked up?" Starr asked.

"The nigga Rich tearin' the mothafuckin' city apart tryin' to find my black ass," Stevie said. "The dude we bodied a couple months ago...Starr, that was Rich's lil' brother—"

"What?!" Starr screamed, snatching the sheets off her body. She nearly dropped her cellphone at that bit of news. "Stevie, don't bullshit with me—"

"Bay, I would never play with you about some shit like that," Stevie stressed. "Damn! We fucked up!"

"No, bitch, *you* fucked up!" Starr corrected her. "Why you have us murk the nigga if you knew he was Rich's brother? You *did* know, right?" she asked.

"No. I just found out," Stevie lied. She didn't want to reveal that she'd actually set Starr up. She knew damn well that Cartier was Rich's brother. She just didn't give a fuck. She also didn't consider the consequences of her ruthless actions.

"Fuck, Stevie!" Starr yelled, raking a hand through her hair. "What the hell?"

"Please, Starr...don't be mad at me. I don't want you to hate me. I fucked up...but I really need you right now."

"Okay, okay. Just calm down," Starr told her. "Look, I gotta lil' spot out here in Lancaster. Why don't you just come out here and lay low—"

"No, you ain't hearin' me, Starr," Stevie cut her off. "When I say this nigga Rich been rippin' the city apart lookin' for me, I mean that shit without the slightest ounce of exaggeration. Wherever the fuck I go the mothafucka gon' find me eventually," she said. "Starr, I'm scared. I can't sleep. I can't eat. I done lost a ton of weight. I can't even take a shit without thinking the nigga gon' kick the door in on me and blow my fuckin' head off. Starr, this ain't no way to live. And I can't run forever..."

"Well, what are you gonna do?" Starr asked.

Stevie ran a hand over her weary face. She couldn't believe what she was about to say. "I'ma have to get at that nigga before he get at me."

"What?" Starr asked, obviously confused. She wanted to be sure she was hearing Stevie correctly. "What are you saying?"

Stevie hesitated. "I'm sayin' I'ma have to kill the nigga."

"*Kill Rich Keys*?!" Starr repeated skeptically. "*Thee* Rich Keys?! Stevie, you know how many connects this nigga got? The type of moves he can make? Bitch, we ain't talkin' 'bout just any ole lame ass nigga—"

"Starr, I know. I know," Stevie stressed. "And that's why I'm positive I can't do this shit on my own...I need your help."

Starr exhaled deeply upon hearing that. Her life was finally beginning to look up—until Stevie suddenly resurfaced out of nowhere.

Starr sighed in frustration as she mulled over the decision. She knew the best thing to do in this situation was to hang up on Stevie's deceitful ass. Instead she asked, "What do you need me to do?"

Stevie paused. "Call Diamond..."

***

"Harder. Harder, Diamond. Damn, how many times I have to tell ya ass?" Bruce complained.

"Well, my bad. I'm just scared I'm gonna hurt you."

"Diamond, how many times I gotta tell you, you ain't gon' hurt me."

"Okay then." Diamond gently pressed the heel of her bare foot deep into Bruce's scrotum.

"*Mmm.* That feels so good," Bruce moaned in delight.

Bruce was an ole fat weird ass motherfucker who took pleasure in violence. He enjoyed everything from being slapped, choked, spit on, and having his balls stepped on.

"Call me a piece of shit," Bruce begged.

Diamond applied more pressure onto Bruce's scrotum. "You like that you piece of shit? You nasty motherfucker!"

"Ooh, yeah. I love when you talk dirty."

Suddenly, Diamond's cellphone rang, interrupting the twisted sex session she and Bruce had going on.

"Don't answer it," Bruce quickly said. He was enjoying himself far too much to stop.

"I have to," Diamond told him, walking over towards the nightstand.

If the caller was LaVelle he'd flip if Diamond didn't answer his phone call. After all, he was the one who paid for the very hotel room that she turned her various tricks in.

The moment Diamond saw the number displayed on the caller ID she did an automatic double take. She didn't expect to hear from Starr anytime soon. Not after the scandalous shit she'd done to her best friend.

Taking a deep breath, Diamond pressed answer and placed the phone against her ear. "Hello?"

"Look, the only reason I'm even calling your two-faced ass is because Stevie needs your help. And as much as she hurt me, I still care about her."

Starr was talking greasy, but Diamond would be lying if she said it wasn't good to hear her old friend's voice. However, her pride wouldn't permit her to admit it.

"So? What the hell that got to do with me?" Diamond asked.

"It has *everything* to do with you," Starr told her. "We need to talk..."

11

Diamond, Starr, and Stevie sat in awkward silence inside of Diamond's hotel room, staring at suspiciously at one another.

Starr sat on the edge of Diamond's bed. Stevie sat across from her in a chair. Starr tried her best to keep from goggling at her ex-girlfriend, but she'd be lying to herself if she said Stevie didn't look sexy as hell right then. Just being in Stevie's presence had her pussy jumping and yearning to be tasted. No one gave head quite like Stevie. She was a master pro at the shit and she knew it.

Stevie ran a hand through her short curly and released a deep sigh. Her hair had grown out since she hadn't gotten a haircut in weeks. Being half-black and half-white, she actually had a really good grade of hair. Baby hairs aligned her edges giving away her mixed heritage.

Stevie was the first one to break the silence. "All I wanna fuckin' know is how the nigga, Rich even know it was me," she said. "I mean, he had no damn idea. I stood in this nigga's face and looked him dead in the eye and I could *see* that he didn't suspect me. He didn't put the pieces together himself. Someone told him."

Starr and Stevie simultaneously looked in Diamond's direction. She immediately looked down at her feet, not wanting to meet their intense gazes.

Stevie then shifted her gaze to Starr. Her heart melted when their eyes met. It wasn't until then that she realized just how much she truly missed Starr. Stevie's sentiments quickly faded when she remembered that Starr had broken her promise.

"So I'm guessin' you told Diamond, right? About us killin' Cartier?"

Starr shrugged. "I had to tell someone, aight. The shit was eating at my conscience."

Stevie grimaced, and turned to face Diamond. "So if me, you, and Starr are the only ones who know the truth about Cartier then how the fuck did Rich find out, Diamond?" she asked. "I damn sure wouldn't have choked. And Starr don't even kick it with the nigga."

"So ya'll think I told him? I would never tell him no shit like that," Diamond lied. "What type of person ya'll think I am?"

"A backstabber," Starr answered smugly.

"Diamond, we're all here in the open. Just be real with your shit. Did you tell the nigga or not?" Stevie asked sternly. There was a humorless expression on her face.

"No. I didn't tell him," Diamond continued to lie.

"Bitch, you lyin'!" Stevie screamed, jumping out her seat and charging towards Diamond.

Before Diamond could defend herself, Stevie wrapped both of her hands around Diamond's throat and proceeded to strangle her in the lounge chair she sat in. "You told the nigga!" she screamed, spittle flying from her mouth. "Why you fuckin' lyin', hoe?!"

Starr quickly hopped off the bed and ran to break up the altercation. "Stevie, chill!" she yelled. "Somebody gon' call the police!" She tried her best to pull Stevie off Diamond. "Let her go. Maybe she ain't tell Rich. Maybe he found out some other way."

Stevie slowly loosened her grip around Diamond's neck, and reluctantly backed off although she wanted to beat the truth out of her ass.

"Believe what you want but I know what's up, Starr," Stevie said, looking directly in Diamond's eyes.

Diamond rubbed her neck and relaxed in the lounge chair. "Bitch, if you ever put your hands on me again—"

"What?! You gon' do what?" Stevie stepped towards her, but Starr quickly jumped between the two.

"Come on ya'll," Starr said. "Fall back. Right now ain't the time for this extra shit. What we need to be doing is trying to figure out how we're going to handle this situation."

Stevie's nostrils flared as she paced back and forth in anger. Her fists were clenched tightly and she wanted nothing more than to fold Diamond's lying ass.

"Whatever, man." Stevie walked back towards her chair and plopped down in the seat.

Now that the heated situation had finally deescalated, Starr walked back over to the bed and sat back down on the mattress. She was just about to speak when suddenly her cellphone rang.

Pulling out her Droid, she checked the caller ID and noticed it was Fame. "Hello?" she answered.

"Bitch, where the fuck you at? Why you ain't at home? And how many times I gotta tell yo' ass to let me know when you leavin'?" Fame lashed out.

He was coming at her like she was a child and he was her over-protective parent. Controlling was an understatement when it came to Fame. He had to know every move she made and everything she did. She couldn't even take a shit without him breathing down her neck. Starr was used to his petty temper tantrums. Fame was nothing more than a big ass, overgrown kid.

"Fame, I'm busy right now—"

"Check this, for every ten minutes you ain't here I'ma start burnin' shit," he warned her. "You better bring yo' ass home now or those Louboutins I just brought you gon' be the first thing to go!"

Starr sighed in frustration. "Come on, Fame. Don't be like that. I'm handling business. I'll be back as soon as I can—"

"Bitch, you got ten minutes!" he said before disconnecting the call.

Starr ignored his threat and continued with her conversation as if Fame hadn't just called. "So how're we gon' do this shit?" she asked, looking from Stevie to Diamond.

"And why do ya'll need me?" Diamond spoke up. "I ain't have shit to do with ya'll murkin' Cartier—"

"I swear if some more dumb shit come out your mouth, I'ma hit you in it."

"Bitch, you gon' stop comin' at me like shit's sweet!"

"Ya'll chill!" Starr demanded. "We gettin' off task with the petty shit." She turned towards Diamond. "Look, you were the closest to the nigga since you were intimate with him."

"Yeah, but what does that have to do with anything?" Diamond asked.

"Fuck beating around the bush," Stevie chimed in. "Diamond, you gon' have to start fuckin' with him again."

"What?! Are you crazy?" Diamond questioned. "And anyway how did you even know that me and Rich weren't kickin' it anymore?"

"The streets talk," Stevie simply said.

"I am not going back to that man. I probably got as good of a rep with him as you," she said.

"What do you mean?" Starr asked.

Diamond didn't want to tell them about her trying to rob the infamous Rich Keys so she kept that bit of information to herself. "We just didn't end on good terms, aight? That's all I'ma say."

"Well, bitch, you better make it up to that nigga," Stevie said. "Put on a good act to get him back. You're an expert at fooling people—"

"And what the fuck is that supposed to mean? You calling me fake or some shit?"

Stevie shrugged nonchalantly. "Hey, if the shoe fits wear it."

Starr was just about to tell them to knock it off when her cellphone suddenly rang. She knew it was Fame without even having to look at the caller ID, but she went ahead and answered it anyway.

"Fame, you're really tripping on me. I told you I'll be home in a minute—"

"This purple dress I brought you last week is next!"

"Come on, Fame. Chill! You know I love that dress!"

"Too late," he said, tossing the $300 dress into the trash fire he had set. "You got another ten minutes before I burn something else. I'm not fuckin' around with you." With that said he disconnected the call.

Stevie rolled her eyes in jealousy. She hated to see another person sweating the woman who still held the key to her heart. "You done?" she asked, her tone dripping with sarcasm.

"Yeah. My fault." Starr looked over at Diamond and an uncomfortable thought came to mind. She couldn't help but wonder why her best friend and girlfriend would betray her in such a manner. "So...how'd it end up happening?" she suddenly asked. "You and Stevie fucking? How did it happen?"

Diamond shifted nervously in her seat before glancing at Stevie.

"Man, I don't wanna talk about that shit, Starr. It ain't even got nothin' to do with what's goin' on right now."

"I just listened to you and Diamond bicker for twenty minutes about some irrelevant shit, but I can't ask a simple question. I *wanna* talk about it," Starr pressed. "I wanna know—no, I *need* to know."

"Like I said, I don't wanna talk about that shit," Stevie repeated sternly.

Starr then turned towards Diamond. "Well, maybe *you* can tell me, Diamond...since you were supposedly *so* anti-lesbian. Remember that?"

Diamond opened her mouth to respond, but Starr's cellphone went off for the third time.

Saved by the bell, Diamond thought to herself.

"Hello?" Starr answered in an irritated tone. She was sick of Fame's shenanigans. They hadn't even been kicking it that long and he was already tripping.

"Bitch, where the fuck you at?!" Fame hollered. "You finna make me come and look for yo' ass. Starr I ain't the mothafuckin' one!"

"Would you just relax, Fame? I told you I'm handling business."

"Bitch, lemme find out you fuckin' with another nigga!"

Immediately, Stevie jumped out her seat, finally losing her cool. After stomping over towards Starr, she rudely snatched the cellphone out her hand.

"Look, nigga, beat it. Aight?" Stevie snapped on Fame. "My bitch don't even like dick. She likes pussy! So kill yaself you lame fuck!" She quickly hung up the phone before Fame could respond.

"Stevie?!" Starr screamed. "You realize I might be homeless now fucking around with you?"

Stevie sucked her teeth. "Man, fuck that insecure ass nigga," she said dismissively. Starr's cellphone started ringing again, but Stevie tossed it onto Diamond's bed. "We ain't got time for that fuck boy right now. We need to figure out what we're gonna do about this Rich situation."

12

Starr pulled into the empty Gas USA located a few blocks from Diamond's hotel. She needed some cigarillos and a few snacks to hold the trio over after they finished smoking. There was so much tension in the hotel room that one could cut a knife through it. Starr only hoped Stevie and Diamond didn't kill each other while she was out.

The brisk night air blew through Starr's half mane as she walked towards the twenty-four hour gas store.

Ding-Ding.

The bell above the door chimed indicating Starr's entrance. She looked over towards the register but didn't see the cashier in sight.

"Gimme one second. I'll be right with you," the male clerk said with his back facing Starr.

Since traffic was slow in the gas station, he decided to do some much-needed stocking and cleaning up.

The moment the store clerk turned towards Starr, the two immediately did an automatic double take.

"Antoine?" Starr asked, surprised that he'd even be working there. "How...I'm...I didn't expect to you see here."

"I didn't expect to see you again. Period," he added.

The look on his face said that he wasn't all too pleased to see her, but inside his heart was doing backflips. He just didn't know how to balance out his feelings. Apart of him wanted to hate Starr for dipping out on him the way she did, especially since he was really digging her. Then there was the part of him that wanted to grab her and hold her.

"I...what are you doing working here?" Starr asked. She instantly regretted it the moment it slipped through her lips.

"I dropped out of school," Antoine said flatly.

Starr was shocked to hear that. "You dropped out of school? Why—I mean you seemed so happy the last time we spoke."

Antoine grimaced. "A lot has happened since the last time we spoke..." He hated to admit it but Starr looked sexy as shit. She'd even gotten a little thicker since the last time he saw her, but the added weight looked damn good.

Starr would have to be a fool or blind to not notice his uptight body language. He wasn't acting like himself. He was distant and cold. "Look, Antoine," she began. "I know—"

"Starr, you don't owe me an explanation. You made your decision and it is what it is," he said. "You don't owe me shit."

"But I feel like I *do* owe you an explanation," Starr argued. "If the shoe was on the other foot I'd want one. To be honest, I just didn't want you caught up in my bullshit. I didn't wanna put you in the middle..."

Antoine chuckled. *"Put me in the middle?"* he repeated skeptically. "Starr, I was involved deeper than you knew," he told her, his statement of course having double meanings. "But it doesn't even matter now. That's the past and it doesn't have anything to do with what's goin' on right now. You're obviously happy. You're lookin' good and healthy so I'm guessin' you gettin' treated right. That's really all that's important. *Your* happiness."

Starr felt like shit. She never knew words meant to be kind could sound so hurtful. "Antoine, I—"

"Look, no offense, but I ain't really tryin' to talk about this no more. I need to get back to my job." With that said, Antoine turned and headed towards the cash register.

Starr contemplated leaving and hitting up another gas store since Antoine was giving her the third degree. However, she couldn't blame him after the unexpected way she had bounced on him.

Without warning, Starr reached for Antoine's arm and gently pulled him towards her. "Antoine..."

"Come on, Starr. Chill. I gotta get back to my job—"

"Boy, shut up and kiss me..."

Starr didn't have to ask twice. Antoine eagerly crushed his lips against hers, and for the moment forgot all about Stevie shooting him underneath the bridge over Starr.

Starr wrapped her arms around Antoine's neck as she stood on her tip toes. Antoine held firmly onto Starr's tiny waist as the two indulged in a passion-filled kiss.

Sensuality quickly turned into aggression as the two went at it right in the middle of the empty store.

Starr backed Antoine against the nearest shelf, accidentally knocking a few items onto the floor. His rough hands slid up her shirt, caressing the smoothness of her back. When he reached her bra, he unhooked it, freeing her petite breasts.

"Let's get off the camera," Antoine whispered in between eager kisses.

In one swift movement, he lifted Starr up. She anxiously wrapped her toned legs around his waist.

Antoine accidentally bumped into the chips rack, knocking a few bags of Doritos onto the floor as he carried Starr to the back of the store.

Antoine anxiously kicked open the door to the small office/maintenance closet. The room was no bigger than a jail cell with an old wooden desk and a tiny tube television that showed the store's camera footage in black and white. There were a few shelves on either side of the room that stored cleaning supplies, and in the farthest corner of the office was the heavy steel safe where he dropped funds periodically.

Carrying Starr with one arm, he used his free hand to swipe the items off the desk before placing her on top of it.

"You're so wild," Starr giggled.

"I missed you," Antoine admitted.

"I missed you too."

"Oh, really?" he asked. "Show me..."

Starr seductively bit her bottom lip as she proceeded to slowly unbutton his pants.

***

Stevie carefully removed several seeds from the weed she'd purchased earlier that day. The silence in the hotel room was unnerving so she decided to finally break it. "Man...I'm sorry about putting my hands on you," she apologized, looking over at Diamond.

Diamond sat in the lounge chair with her knees drawn to her chest while playing Angry Birds on her cellphone. She looked up long enough to roll her eyes at Stevie.

"I mean it," Stevie stressed. "I fucks with you. And I'm sorry for accusing you of telling Rich about that shit. I should have known you wouldn't stoop that low."

Diamond looked up at Stevie. It was funny how she truly believed she knew the type of person Diamond was. In all actuality, Stevie didn't have the slightest damn clue. She remained silent as she listened to Stevie speak.

"We might've not always saw eye to eye— but we shared something special that means more than whatever the fuck you and Rich had goin' on."

Diamond burst into laughter. "*Something special*?!" she repeated sarcastically. "So you sucked on my pussy...what's so special about that?"

"Bitch, you can sit over there and front if you want to, but you and I both know what's up."

Diamond smirked and shook at her head at Stevie. The girl was nothing more than a nut and there she sat thinking it was something more to it.

There was an uncomfortable silence between both women.

"So," Stevie began. "Why you here? In this hotel and shit?"

"What you think?" Diamond asked. "Tryin' to get it how I live."

"By doin' what?"

"Hell, whatever I gotta do."

Stevie sucked her teeth and shook her head. "Damn. Don't you ever get tired of that ratchet shit, Diamond?"

Diamond placed her phone in her lap and sat upright in her seat. Looking Stevie dead in the eyes she said, "I been fucking niggas for money since I was fifteen years old. That's all I know. I ain't with that nine to five shit. Why would I break a sweat behind some fryer when all I'll ever need is right between my legs?"

"Don't that shit ever get old?" Stevie asked. "I mean look where the fuck you at?" she gestured towards their surroundings. "In a dingy ass hotel like some low-class prostitute. Diamond, you better than this shit and you know it."

Diamond tossed her hands up. "Well, how else am I gonna get money?" she asked. "Since you think you know every damn thing, answer me that shit."

Stevie continued to break the weed down. "It's funny you ask that," she said. "Because I actually gotta foolproof plan on how we can all make a big come up...and it involves you and Rich..."

***

Antoine roughly turned Starr around and bent her over the old wooden desk. Her bare round ass looked enticing as she patiently waited for him to enter her from behind.

Antoine hurriedly slid out of his jeans. Overseeing the store was the last thing on his mind as he slowly slipped inside of Starr's wet pussy.

"*Ooh*, shit," Starr moaned, arching her back and pushing against his pelvis.

Antoine grabbed both of Starr's arms and held them behind her back as if she were being placed under arrest. With his free hand, he gave her hair a gentle tug.

"Damn! You feel so good in me," Starr whimpered.

"I wanna feel you all the time," Antoine told her. "I wanna wake up and fall asleep in this pussy." He quickly sped his pace up, and grabbed onto Starr's shoulders as his pelvis slapped against her ass. He bent down and trailed his tongue along her back before working his way towards her neck and nibbling on her earlobe. Antoine reached his hand underneath her and massaged her moist clit. "Do you want that?" he asked.

"Yes! Yes!" Starr moaned in pleasure.

Antoine carefully turned Starr around and lifted her upward so that she sat upright on the desk, facing him.

"You are so damn beautiful to me," he whispered.

Starr multi-tasked between kissing Antoine and removing his uniform shirt. Once she pulled it over his head she casually tossed it onto the floor. "I'm sorry," she told him, staring into his penetrating eyes. "I didn't mean to hurt you..."

Antoine cupped her chin and kissed her passionately. "You didn't hurt me," he said. "I hurt myself 'cuz I knew what was up, but I still chose to fall…"

Starr took his hand and placed a soft kiss on the back of it. "I think about you all the time…in case you ever wondered…I do."

A slight smirk tugged at his full lips. "I think about you too, babe."

Starr gradually slid upward and guided his pole inside her. "How much do you think about me?" she asked.

Antoine pushed in harder. "Every day," he admitted.

Starr placed delicate kisses on Antoine's neck and then worked her way downward towards his shoulder…before suddenly stopping at his chest. She curiously stared at the bullet wound scar just beneath his collarbone, and then looked up at Antoine with questioning eyes.

Antoine instantly tensed up as an uncomfortable feeling washed over him. Without warning, he pulled out of Starr and proceeded to dress.

"I think you'd better go," he said, not looking at her.

13

Who got that baddest pussy on the planet...

D-Boys love me, they don't understand it...

Cymphanie groaned in irritation as her cellphone rang. "Ugh! It's too damn early," she complained, snatching the bed sheet off her body. Mumbling obscenities, she reached for her cellphone.

"Hello?!" she answered in an irritated tone.

"Cymph? Did I wake you?" Starr asked in a hush tone.

"Starr? What's up girl?" Cymphanie wiped the sleep from her eyes and sat up in bed.

"Cymph...," Starr paused. "I'm pregnant..."

***

Knock!

Knock!

Knock!

Knock!

Rich immediately placed his newspaper on the table upon the incessant knocking on his front door.

"Would you like me to answer the door?" Lolita, Rich's attractive Spanish chef asked, placing a fresh cup of coffee in front of him.

"Nah, I got it ma," he said, folding the newspaper closed. *This better be good*, he thought.

Rich hoped his boys had gotten word on Stevie's whereabouts. Just thinking about what he'd do to Stevie the moment he got his hands on her had him both anxious and excited. He was absolutely mortified when he discovered the very bitch he'd been feeding had taken his little brother from him. *I'ma make this bitch pay*, he promised himself.

"¿Estás seguro de?"

Rich stood to his feet. "Yeah, I'm sure boo," he answered.

After giving Lolita's large, round ass a firm slap, Rich made his way to the front door where the volume of the knocking had increased. He tightened the sash to the white American Essentials robe he wore and peered through the peephole.

What the hell?

Rich surely didn't expect to see the conniving, backstabbing woman that had effortlessly stolen his heart and run off with it.

Apart of him wanted to let her ass bang on the door, but against his better judgment he went ahead and opened it. "Whatcha ass doin' here, Diamond?" Rich asked nonchalantly.

He wasn't all too pleased with the sight of her standing on his doorstep. She even looked a little ran down. Not like how she looked when he first met her and started dealing with her.

What the fuck she been on, Rich wondered.

Nevertheless, he couldn't deny that he still had feelings for the chick even though she'd straight played his shit.

"I miss you," Diamond confessed. "I wanna come back."

Rich moved to close the door in her face, but Diamond quickly stopped him by placing her hand against it.

"Please...I'm sorry...I fucked up."

"Why the fuck you jump out the car like that?" Rich asked. "And why ain't ya ass been home? You doin' all this suspicious shit like you got somethin' to hide from a nigga." He stepped closer to Diamond. "You ain't got nothin' to hide from me, do you?" he asked with a serious expression on his handsome dark brown face.

"Rich...baby...I was scared," Diamond admitted, searching his eyes for sympathy. Of course she saw none of that shit.

"Bullshit, Diamond. You on one and you know it. How you gon' tell me some shit like that and then bounce? And more importantly, how could ya ass have known for so long and not tell a nigga?" Rich shook his head at her. "My judgment was all fucked up with you."

"No, it wasn't—"

"Let me tell ya ass somethin', Diamond. I'm thirty-two damn years old. I ain't a fuckin' game you can just play with whenever the fuck you feel like it. And I damn sure ain't none of these lame ass fuck niggas you used to. I'm. Not. The. One." Rich paused between each word he said to ensure that Diamond heard him correctly.

Diamond slowly stepped closer to Rich and reached towards his face...

He quickly grabbed her hand, stopping her from caressing his cheek. "Bitch, don't touch me," he sneered. "You lucky I'm even givin' yo ass the benefit of the doubt. I should beat yo' ass."

"You done?" Diamond asked, unfazed by his demeanor. "You done with yo' bad boy tirade?" She reached for his face again, but he didn't stop her that time. Her touch felt so good as she ran her fingers along his jawline. Her hand was so warm and soft. "I know the type of nigga you are," Diamond told him. "I've known since the day I met you. You ain't gotta stress to me what I already know..." She slowly stepped into his home, boldly invading his privacy. Taking him by the arms, she pulled his muscular body into hers. "Let me show you the type of female I can be," she whispered.

"You showed me already," Rich said, backing away. It was obvious that he was still hurt.

Diamond tightened her grip around Rich, refusing to let him go. "Let me show you the *real* me," she pleaded. "I fucked up by going back to my old ways...but I promise I can make you love me again—"

"What makes you think I even loved ya ass in the first place?"

Diamond gently framed Rich's face with her hands and stood on her tip toes to kiss him.

Initially, Rich was with it up until she slipped her tongue inside his mouth. He immediately pulled away from her, putting some much needed space between them.

Rich's unexpected gesture didn't faze Diamond in the least. She reached for him and slowly pulled him close to her. The second time she kissed him he didn't fight it. He willingly allowed her to explore his mouth as she tugged on his dick through his robe.

Suddenly, Rich pulled away and slammed Diamond against the foyer wall. He then wrapped a large hand around her throat. "This right here...what we doin'...you don't run this shit. You don't run me. You got it?"

Diamond nodded her head.

Rich then loosened his grip. "You got that shit?" he repeated, looking her dead in the eyes.

"Yes, daddy," Diamond answered in a small voice.

Rich then pinned his body against Diamond's and crushed his thick lips against hers. She anxiously wrapped her arms around his neck. Her pussy throbbed, yearning to feel him inside her. It had been too damn long.

Diamond moaned in pleasure as Rich gently nibbled on the soft flesh of her neck. His hands eagerly explored her body through her clothing. Unashamed, the two made out in the foyer of his mini mansion as if they'd never wronged each other.

"If you ever run away from me again I'ma fuck you up. You hear me?" Rich asked in between aggressive kisses.

"Yes, baby," Diamond breathed heavily.

Rich quickly snatched Diamond off the wall and lifted her up. She wrapped her thick thighs around his waist and continued her kissing frenzy.

Rich carried Diamond into the master bedroom. When he made it inside he tossed her onto his mattress like a rag doll. She wasted no time as she quickly undressed and tossed her clothing onto the plush carpet.

"How do you want me?" Diamond asked, biting her lip.

Rich rubbed his goatee and stared at her nude body. Every curve was perfectly proportioned. She was beautiful without even trying. Or maybe she wasn't even all that...but just in his mind she was.

"You ain't shit...and I know you ain't shit," Rich said in a low tone. "So how the fuck could you be flawless?"

Diamond smiled and seductively crawled to the edge of the bed where she undid his robe. When his terry robe loosely dropped around his ankles, Diamond grabbed his rigid dick and stuffed it inside her oral cavity.

Rich groaned in pleasure and leaned his head back. "Damn..."

Diamond greedily sucked his pole, and with a free hand, gently massaged his scrotum. She knew exactly how to make a nigga fall in love all over again.

"Shit, Diamond," Rich moaned.

She gave him the sloppiest, wettest head he'd ever gotten in his entire life. A few minutes ago Rich was ready to choke Diamond's ass out and now she had him like putty inside her small hand. If Cartier was alive he'd call his a big brother a damn fool for taking Diamond's treacherous ass back, but Rich would be damned if it wasn't something addictive about her.

"Damn, Diamond. You keep this shit up you gon' make a nigga cum," Rich said.

"Not before I get mine," Lolita whispered, wrapping her arms around his neck from behind.

***

Starr and Cymphanie were seated at a booth enjoying their lunch at Rigsby's Kitchen in Columbus, Ohio when Starr recapped her various symptoms.

"My period was light for a few months and then it just completely disappeared," Starr explained. "At first I didn't think anything of it...I just thought it was one of my weird cycles—"

"Now that you mention it I do remember you throwing up that morning at my crib."

"Right," Starr agreed. "But other than that I really didn't feel any different—"

"I ain't tryin' to be funny, but you did put on a lil' weight since the last time I saw you," Cymphanie said.

Starr paused and rolled her eyes at her older cousin. Cymphanie never missed an opportunity to point out someone else's flaws, but she was the most dysfunctional motherfucker Starr knew.

"Thanks for noticing," Starr said, her tone dripping with sarcasm. "Anyway last night I went and got a test from Rite Aid. I didn't even wait until I got home...I pissed on the stick right outside of my car, girl," she admitted.

Cymphanie took a bite out of the Canlis salad and shook her head in disbelief. "Damn...I ain't know you and Fame were going at it like *that*. Got damn, Starr. You ain't even known the nigga a whole two months and you already lettin' him swim raw? I mean, I know he got you your own spot, but damn—"

"That's the thing, Cymphanie," Starr cut her off. "Me and Fame strap up every time. And he's anal about that shit, girl."

"So did you fuck anybody before Fame raw?" Cymphanie asked. "Shit, now that I think back to it, you were throwing up before you even met the nigga, Fame."

Starr shook her head. "No—I mean there was *one* guy, but even we strapped up."

Cymphanie stared at her cousin with a sympathetic expression. She gently placed her hand on top of Starr's. "Cuz...you gotta go find out how far along you are."

14

"Let me stop and get some gas real quick," Cymphanie said, pulling her freshly washed BMW into the AM/PM gas station.

Starr had met Cymphanie at her crib, and left her whip there so that the two of them could ride together.

After parking at pump two, Cymphanie killed the engine. She turned to face Starr. "You want something from inside?" she asked.

"No. I'm good. Thanks anyway."

Cymphanie placed her hand over Starr's stomach. "You sure, mama? The baby might wanna snack."

Starr sucked her teeth and pushed Cymphanie's hand away. "Girl, bye," she laughed.

Cymphanie giggled and unfastened her seat belt. "You better start getting used to being called mama," she said, climbing out the car.

"Get me a bag of white cheddar popcorn!" Starr hollered. She was unsure if Cymphanie had even heard her since she had already slammed the door and walked off.

Starr relaxed in her seat as she allowed her mind to drift. She couldn't help but replay the events from last night over and over in her mind. It all felt so surreal.

Damn. Why did he flip like that?

Starr then reflected on the way Antoine had kissed her and touched her. She replayed the things he'd said. Right about now she wanted nothing more than to be in his arms. Starr then thought about the possibility of being pregnant by Antoine.

How would he react if I tell him?

Antoine and Fame had been the only two men she'd slept with since Stevie so between the two of them it had to be either one or the other. Of course, Starr hoped it was indeed Antoine's.

Although the time she'd spent with Antoine was minimal, Starr couldn't help but relish the time they'd shared. Every time she saw him he made her heart flutter without even trying. It was a feeling she couldn't explain or understand for that matter.

"I need to see him again. But first I gotta know for sure," Starr told herself.

She watched as Cymphanie exited the gas store and made her way back towards the car. Unfortunately, she was empty-handed meaning she hadn't heard Starr's request. Either that or she'd simply ignored her.

Every man at the gas station's eyes was fastened to her fat ass as she sashayed extra hard in the Vintage wide leg pants she wore. Cymphanie was the shit and she knew it.

"You lil' mothafuckin' bitch!"

Starr's eyes bulged in their sockets as she watched some random dude run up and punch the shit out of Cymphanie!

Her cousin hit the pavement at the same time Starr jumped out the car.

"You thought you were just gon' steal from me and get away with it, hoe?!" Devon screamed. "Where's my mothafuckin' jewelry?!"

Cymphanie lay pathetically on the ground, cradling her bloodied nose as she stared up at Devon in horror. This was the first time her scandalous ways had come back to haunt her.

Starr ran up and shoved Devon with all her might yet he barely moved.

"Nigga, you fuckin' crazy?!" Starr screamed.

Devon surprised Starr when he snatched her up by her throat. "Bitch, you wanna get fucked up too?" he spat.

"Aye, man! Chill! These some mothafuckin' females!" A male bystander and his friend pulled Devon off Starr.

"Nigga, get the fuck off me!" Devon yelled, aggressively pulling away from the two nondescript men restraining him. He then pointed a finger at Cymphanie. "Bitch, the next time I see you I ain't just gon' steal on ya ass. I'ma kill you," he threatened.

With that said, Devon walked towards his car parked at pump five. He hopped inside his truck and peeled off, not realizing the gas nozzle still inside his gas tank. The nozzle and hose instantly ripped off the pump, but Devon was too pissed off to notice or care. All he could think about was what he'd do to Cymphanie the next time he saw her.

***

Cymphanie used her shoulder to hold her cellphone against her ear as she dabbed her bloodied nose with a used napkin. She stared at her reflection in the car visor mirror and was on the verge of tears.

Cymphanie sat parked in her car at the store right up the street from where she lived. She was too afraid to even go home for fear that Devon might follow her and discover where she resided.

The line rang several times before Rich finally answered in a muffled tone. An epic sex session with two beautiful women had briefly put him out of commission. "Hello?"

"Rich...baby...I wanna come back. No, I need to come back..."

Rich yawned, pulled the sheets off him, and climbed out his bed.

Diamond groaned, but remained asleep.

Padding barefoot, Rich walked over to the double French doors that led to his patio. "Why's that?" he asked in a nonchalant tone, stepping out onto the patio. He closed the doors behind him. The patio overlooked the beautiful pool and deck in his backyard.

Cymphanie wouldn't dare tell Rich about the dangerous life she led. Truth be told, she simply wanted to come back because she needed protection. Devon was the first, but it'd only be a matter of time before every nigga Cymphanie ever wronged came looking for her ass.

"I was attacked today," she told Rich. "I was pumping my gas and this guy ran up on me and attacked me. He'd been stalking me for a while now but I never thought he'd put his hands on me," Cymphanie lied. "My cousin, Starr was with me. She tried to stop him but—"

"Hold up. Did you just say Starr?" Rich cut her off. How could he forget the name? He rubbed his goatee and replayed Diamond's words over in his mind. "Quick question. She got a girlfriend named Stevie?"

"Yeah—well...Stevie's her ex. Why?" Cymphanie asked, clearly confused. "What's up?"

"Where does Starr stay?"

15

Starr closed the front door behind herself after entering her home. It was unnaturally quiet and there wasn't a single light on in the home. After locking the door, she flicked on the nearest light switch which lit up the foyer.

"Fame?" Starr called out, stepping further inside her home. "Fame, you here?"

His Porsche Panamera was parked in the driveway so Starr figured he was at her crib.

Just then Fame stepped into the hallway. He was shirtless and wore an expressionless look on his face. Underneath his nostrils was white residue left over from the line he'd just done. Fame had been going in on the coke since Starr's brief absence.

Unfortunately, as a child Fame had suffered from abandonment issues. As a teen he'd been diagnosed with possessive personality disorder, and as an adult he'd transformed into an overly insecure, dominating control freak. It was because of that unattractive quality that Fame couldn't keep a girl longer than a month.

Starr, on the other hand, was a bit more patient, considering she was used to dealing with Stevie who wasn't too far off from being a lot like Fame.

"Where the fuck you been?" Fame asked in a surprisingly calm tone.

Starr kicked her shoes off. "I had to go to Cleveland to handle some business."

Fame slowly approached Starr. "Why didn't you ask me if it was cool for you to go?"

Starr rolled her eyes. *Here he goes with this shit.* "Boy, I'm not in the mood for this right now," she said dismissively. "Last time I checked, I was an adult. Besides...I'm too tired to argue with you right now."

"*Tired*?!" Fame repeated. "Why the fuck you so tired and what the hell were you doing last night? Were you with another nigga? I'm not good enough for you?" He berated Starr with questions and accusations at the same time. "It's the damn catheter, ain't it?"

"Fame, no! What are you talking about? I don't care about your catheter—"

"Well, why the fuck you act like you can't tell me where you were last night?"

Starr tried to walk around Fame, but he suddenly pinned her against the wall. "You don't appreciate a nigga, huh? Is that what it is?" he asked. "Ya cousin had you sleepin' on her mothafuckin' couch and I put ya ass in a brand new townhome. This is how you treat me?"

"Fame, you're high...and you're trippin'," Starr shook her head.

"You supposed to be my bitch but you're just like the rest...and who was that on ya damn phone last night?"

Starr turned her head away and rolled her eyes.

It was then that Fame noticed the ugly purplish bruise on the side of Starr's neck.

"The fuck?!" Fame hollered. "So you *did* fuck another nigga—hickies on ya neck and shit!"

"What are you talking about?" Starr asked with much attitude.

Little did Fame know, the mark on Starr's neck was from Devon choking her, but Fame was far too insecure to believe her if she told him.

"I didn't fuck anyone, Fame! Now would you please get out of my way—"

"Take them panties off!" Fame demanded.

"Wh—What?" Starr stammered.

"Bitch, you heard me! Take them mothafuckin' panties off! I wanna see 'em!" he yelled. "I wanna smell 'em too!"

Starr pushed past Fame. "Nigga, you are seriously trippin'! What is you on?"

Fame quickly latched onto Starr's arm and slammed her against the wall so hard that the back of her head created a dent in it.

"Take your mothafuckin' panties off...or I'ma take 'em off for you," he threatened in a low tone.

Tears streamed down Starr's reddened cheeks.

What the hell did I get myself into, she wondered.

16

Starr took her time as she unfastened and unzipped her jeans. She felt absolutely ridiculous standing in the hallway of her home being berated like she was a damn teenager instead of a grown ass woman.

Fame stood hovering over her like a wild animal. His nostrils flared wildly as he impatiently waited for Starr to hand over her panties.

"This is ridiculous," Starr told him. "You know that, right?"

Fame didn't reply as he watched Starr gradually pull her jeans down her legs. After stepping out of them, she fumbled with easing down her panties down.

"Look, I ain't got all day to play with ya ass!" Fame snapped, reaching for Starr's panties.

"No, I got it! I got it!" Starr argued.

"Well, hurry the fuck up! Playin' around and shit."

Starr was just about to pull her panties down when the frantic banging on the front door suddenly stopped her.

"Who the fuck is that?" Fame asked angrily.

Starr sniffled and wiped her nose. "I don't know," she mumbled.

Fame sulked as he made his way towards the front door. Starr quickly used that time to pull on her jeans.

Fame didn't bother looking through the peephole before he swung the front door open.

WHAP!

The butt of a 9mm crashed into the bridge of his nose.

"*Aahh*! Shit!" Fame cried out in pain. He immediately hit the floor after the unexpected blow. "The fuck, man?!"

Starr screamed as three masked men dressed in all black ran inside her home. The moment they saw her, they ran straight towards her!

Before Starr could figure out what the hell was going on, the masked intruders roughly seized her...

***

Stevie took an aggressive pull on the Mild and every so often glanced out her car windows. Her nerves had been extremely on the edge lately. She couldn't go anywhere or do anything without looking over her shoulder.

Rich had the entire city on lookout for her as if she were a missing child. Stevie had never been so paranoid in her twenty-four years of living.

Dialing Starr's number for the fifth time that evening, Stevie released a sigh of irritation. As expected she didn't receive an answer.

"What the hell is this bitch on?" she asked herself. Annoyed with Starr's sudden absence, Stevie went ahead and dialed Diamond's number.

"I told you not to call me. I'll call *you*," Diamond said in a hush tone.

"Can that shit, Starr ain't answerin' her phone," Stevie told her. "I've been blowin' her ass up. She said she was going back to the crib to grab some clothes and she'd be back."

Diamond sucked her teeth. "Maybe she gotta change of heart, Stevie. I mean shit, could you blame her? You need her...it ain't the other way around..."

"Nah, Starr wouldn't do me like that," Stevie argued. "If she say she gon' be there for me, she gon' be there for me. We've been through our share of bullshit but we got history. She still cares about me...I know it..."

Diamond shook her head. "Keep tellin' yaself that."

Stevie sucked her teeth. "Man, whatever. Is the nigga, Rich around?"

"No, he actually just left."

"Well, you need to get on your job, and in the meantime I'll figure out what's up with Starr."

"Stevie, how in the hell am I supposed to figure out where Rich keeps his stash?" Diamond asked.

"Hell, follow his ass around. Shit, I don't know. Bitch, that's what you're there to find out," Stevie said before hanging up.

Diamond and Stevie's plan for robbing Rich Keys went into full effect the moment he opened his front door and allowed Diamond entrance.

***

The tan sack covering Starr's head was viciously snatched off. She wasted no time as she eagerly took in her surroundings. The dark, dank room smelled stale, and a single light bulb was the only thing offering illumination. Somewhere in the distance was the constant dripping of water. Starr immediately realized that she was trapped in a basement.

"Mothafuckin' Starr," Rich muttered, looking down at her in disdain.

Starr's eyes darted from Rich to the four goons standing on either side of him. "Why did you bring here, motherfucker? Let me go!" she demanded, rocking back and forth in the wooden chair she was tied to. Her ankles were bound by duct tape to the front legs of the chair and her wrists were tied to the arms.

WHAP!

Rich suddenly slapped the shit out of Starr. "I'm the mothafucka in charge right now!" he yelled. "You hear me? I run this shit! If any mothafuckin' body gon' be barkin' orders, it's me? Do I make my damn self clear?"

Blood trailed down Starr's chin from the wound on her bottom lip. Rich had busted her shit wide open. Hesitantly, she nodded her head.

"I said do I make myself clear?" he repeated in a more stern tone.

Starr looked him dead in the eyes. "Yes...Rich," she answered through clenched teeth.

Rich looked surprised. "Oh, so you *do* know who I am?" he said. "And from the tone of ya voice you sound like you ain't too surprised you're here right now. So, I'm guessin' you know why then...?"

Starr remained silent as she stared angrily at Rich.

Rich folded his tatted, cocky arms across his chest. "A lil' birdie told me you had something to do with my brother's death," he continued. "Bitch, you better hope for yo' sake that the mothafucka had their story wrong..."

Tears streamed down Starr's reddened cheeks, but she tried her best to look tough. "I was there...but I didn't kill him—"

"How did it happen?" Rich said in a low tone, barely above a whisper.

"Wh—What?" Starr stammered.

"Tell me how the mothafuckin' shit happened!" Rich barked.

Starr jumped at the loud, threatening tone of his voice. "Okay," she whimpered. "Me and him—"

"You and *who*?" Rich asked, clearly agitated.

"Me and Cartier were sitting in his car choppin' it up...flirting, making out and shit...and my girl ran up to his car window," Starr explained timidly. "She put the gun to his head and told him to give her his money and jewelry—but Cartier didn't step down easily...he fought back..."

Rich nodded his head in admiration, proud that his little brother hadn't gone out like a sucker. "And then what happened?"

"He jumped out the car and started whuppin' my girl's ass—"

"Stevie," Rich cut her off. "You might as well just say Stevie. I already know what's up. You ain't protectin' shit...and for your sake you should be more worried about your own well-being..."

Starr swallowed the large lump that had formed in her throat. "Stevie...he started whuppin' Stevie's ass," she nervously continued. "I...I got out the car to try to...st—stop him...but I couldn't. I ended up getting his attention off of Stevie for a little while...long enough for her to get up. He—Cartier shot me in the leg,"

Starr was hoping to earn some sympathy points. Of course, she didn't get any. Rich and his goons remained stone-faced as they listened to Starr's disturbing play-by-play on how Cartier had been killed.

"When he wasn't paying attention, Stevie smashed him in the back of a head with a brick," Starr confessed.

Rich exhaled deeply as rage washed over him. His fists clenched tightly as he imagined the damage he'd inflict on Stevie the moment he got his hands on her.

"He—Cartier fell down on the ground after the first blow," Starr continued, unsure if she should go on or not. "But Stevie didn't stop. She kept hitting him over and over in the head with the br—"

Starr's sentence was immediately cut short after Rich knocked her ass out cold in mid-sentence.

17

Antoine lifted the half full bottle of Hennessy to his lips and took a swig. He looked more like a helpless, strung out addict than a man once full of life, goals, and happiness.

Life's a bitch and then you die, Antoine thought to himself.

He'd been kicked off the basketball team, dropped out of college, and moved into some cruddy apartment near downtown Cleveland. Life couldn't have been any worse. It was slowly deteriorating before his very eyes.

Antoine's family and friends had shown their true colors during a moment when he needed their support the most. Everyone loved him when they thought he had a possibility of getting drafted to the Cleveland Cavaliers, but the minute his dream had been shattered they quickly dispersed.

Sometimes family and friends can do you worse than the snakes in the street.

Antoine took another swig from the bottle.

He had nothing and no one, but a crappy part-time job at a gas station and a negative bank account balance.

Life's a bitch and then you die, he said to himself.

Antoine lifted the polished Glock he'd been holding for an entire hour, and placed the barrel of it against his temple...

***

Nadine Keys gently patted a warm wash cloth against an unconscious Starr's forehead. After cooling her down a little, Nadine proceeded to wipe away the dry blood on her mouth and chin.

Starr softly groaned as she slowly came to. Her head throbbed in pain and her jaw was still sore from where Rich had brutally punched her.

The moment Starr's eyes connected with Nadine's, she gasped and jumped. For a moment, Starr had completely forgotten where she was and why she was even there.

"Shh. Shh," Nadine said in a soft, soothing tone.

However, Starr remained silent and afraid as she sat bound to a wooden chair in the basement of Rich's mother's home.

Nadine seemed totally unfazed and unsympathetic towards Starr's fear. She never questioned her son's actions, because she knew everything he did was for a legitimate reason.

Nadine, also known as Mama Keys by family and friends, was one of the most ruthless drug queen pins in the mid-west. She'd had her reign in the early 70s and 80s, but now she lived a lesser enthusiastic life as a normal, everyday person. It was much safer that way.

Starr studied Mama Keys' features. She was a beautiful, older dark-skinned woman that looked to be in her mid-fifties. Her long hair was pulled back into a sleek ponytail and edges were sprinkled with silver. Mama Keys' large brown eyes were listless and cold, yet she had a caring expression on her face.

Starr could tell just from looking at her that she'd had a rough life.

"You must've done something really bad to piss my son off," Mama Keys said, gently wiping the blood off Starr's mouth.

***

Diamond looked stunning in a cobalt lace bandage dress that hugged every curve on her five foot five-inch frame. On her feet was a pair of black Giuseppe platform pumps. Rich had given her money to get her hair and makeup done for tonight's occasion. Dinner at Giovanni's; a classy five-star eatery known for being one of the top romantic restaurants in the Cleveland Metropolitan area.

Rich had his swag on full display wearing a $900 Givenchy sweatshirt, black cargo pants, and a pair of $700 Metal Star Trimmed leather high top sneakers. Every time he stepped out, Rich had to show out and be the center of attention.

"Dinner at a fancy restaurant...Damn, baby. What'd I do to deserve all this?" Diamond smiled. She looked absolutely radiant with her makeup done to perfection and her soft curls bouncing with every gesture she did.

Before Rich could answer, their waiter returned with two glasses of red wine and placed one before each of them. After scribbling down their orders, he hastily left the two to continue their conversation.

"I wanted to put what you said to me earlier to the test," Rich told her.

Diamond's eyebrows furrowed in confusion. "I don't understand, bay."

Rich studied Diamond from across the table. Everything about her was perfect. From her hour glass figure, to her 36 D cup breasts, to her smooth coffee brown skin, she was absolutely flawless.

Rich owned one of the hottest strip clubs in The Land, and out of all the bad ass chicks on his roster Diamond was still the sexiest—and she didn't even work for him.

However, aside from her captivating looks, Diamond was also sneaky, conniving, and disloyal. Once a bitch fucked up in his book it was a wrap. Rich wasn't a firm believer of second chances, but he'd went out on a limb by forgiving Diamond. He was all out of his element by easily letting her back into his life, but damn if she didn't have some good game...and some even better pussy. Rich only hoped he hadn't made the wrong decision.

"When you first stepped foot into my home earlier today, you said 'Let me show you the type of female I am.' You remember saying that shit right?" Rich asked.

Diamond smiled, revealing her perfect set of teeth. "Of course I do."

"Well, tonight I wanna know if you was just blowin' smoke or if you really meant that shit," Rich told her. "I need you to show me the type of female you are."

"I'll do anything for you, bay," Diamond said eagerly. That should have been apparent when she and Lolita gave Rich one of the wildest, passionate threesomes he'd ever experienced in life.

Rich nodded his head in approval. Diamond had said exactly what he wanted to hear. He watched as she took a sip from the wine glass. "LaVelle," he suddenly said. "You know him. Am I right?"

Diamond nearly choked on the expensive red wine. "Yeah. Wh—Why?" she stuttered.

"I'ma need you to introduce us," Rich simply said.

"You want me to introduce you to a surgeon?" Diamond asked, confused by his request.

Rich cackled at her question. "*Surgeon*?!" he repeated. "Baby, I don't know about no surgeon, but the nigga got one of the best coke connects in Ohio."

Diamond couldn't believe that ass-sniffing, nasty ass LaVelle was that dude. He'd told her when he first met her that he was an oral and maxillofacial surgeon. She would have never believed that he was lying.

Reaching across the table, Diamond placed her hand over Rich's. "I'll do whatever it takes to get you to trust me again..."

18

WHAP!

Rich backslapped the shit out of Starr, reopening the wound on her bottom lip, and causing her to accidentally bite down on her tongue.

"Bitch, I'ma ask ya ass one more time," Rich pointed an accusatory finger in Starr's face. "Tell me where the fuck Stevie at!"

Starr leaned over in the chair and spit a mouthful of thick blood onto the dirty basement floor. "Please...," she said in a low tone. "Just let me go..."

WHAP!

Starr's left cheek met the back of Rich's hand. His pinky ring accidentally sliced into the skin just above her eyebrow.

Rich leaned down towards Starr so that they were eye to eye. "That bitch worth dying for?!" he barked, spittle flying from his mouth and spraying her face.

When Starr didn't respond, Rich grabbed a handful of Starr's hair and viciously yanked her head back. This time around they were the only two people in the basement. No goons standing nearby wearing expressionless looks. Just Starr and Rich.

"I asked you a question," Rich said through gritted teeth. "Is that bitch worth dying for?"

"I don't know where she is," Starr cried through swollen lips.

Rich finally released Starr's hair. Gently, he cupped her chin and tilted her face towards his as if he were preparing to kiss her. Looking her dead in the eyes, he said, "I ain't the nigga to fuck with, Starr. If you know anything about me, you oughta know that shit."

Starr sniffled as tears streamed down her cheeks. Blood leaked down the side of her face from the gash above her eyebrow.

"You and this bitch took my brother from me...," Rich continued in a low tone. "Not my cousin...not one of my niggas on the streets...my mothafuckin' brother...my blood."

Starr's bottom lip trembled uncontrollably as she feared what Rich would do to her next.

"I should've killed yo' triflin' ass the moment I got my hands on you, but I'm givin' you a chance to redeem yaself," he told her.

When Starr didn't respond, Rich dug in his back jeans pocket.

Starr instantly jumped, fearful that he was about to pull out a gun. She relaxed a little when she saw him brandish a cellphone...her cellphone to be exact.

"Since you act like you don't know where the fuck she at I guess we gotta go to Plan B." Rich scrolled through Diamond's contacts as if he owned the Droid and immediately located Stevie's number. "I want you to tell her to meet you at Hampton Park at exactly eight o'clock. You got that?"

Starr remained silent as she stared at Rich with hate-filled eyes.

Rich went ahead and dialed the number and placed the cellphone against Starr's ear. The line rang twice before Stevie's raspy voice filled the receiver.

"Starr, where the fuck you been at?!" Stevie yelled. "You had me worried as fuck. I've been waiting for ya ass. Tell me what's the move cuz a bitch sleepin' in her car and shit like a mothafuckin' bum. I need you."

Rich nodded his head towards the phone, indicating for Starr to do her part in setting Stevie up.

Starr gazed into Rich's penetrating eyes. Without warning, she spat a mouthful of blood onto his face.

"Starr? Starr, you there?" Stevie called out.

Rich immediately disconnected the call. He was eerily calm as he slowly wiped the blood off his face. Never in his thirty-two years of living had he ever felt so disrespected. There was nothing more degrading than spitting on someone.

Without a word, Rich replaced Starr's cellphone in the back of his jeans. "I guess that bitch is worth dyin' for, huh?" he asked. "I told you I wasn't the nigga to fuck with...but now I see I'ma have to show ya ass. Bitch, when I'm done with you, you gon' be beggin' me to kill ya ass," Rich promised. "First, I'ma let all my niggas fuck you...and then I'ma starve ya ass periodically—but don't worry, I won't let you die. Believe that." He cackled sadistically. "Nah, I'ma keep ya ass alive so I can repeat the cycle over and over again. And I'ma keep you sober. I ain't gon' put no drugs in you cuz I want you sane and aware of everything that's gon' happen to you." Rich leaned towards Starr. "I'ma watch you slowly lose your mind until you beg me to kill you...until you give up on this pathetic ass shit you call your life."

Suddenly, Starr lost control of her bladder and urinated all over herself. Piss spilled off the chair and splashed onto Rich's expensive designer shoes.

Rich backed away from Starr, looking at her in disgust. "We could've done this shit the easy way, but you chose to do it the hard way..."

"Fuck you," Starr spat.

Initially, Rich seemed unfazed by her stubbornness, but suddenly he lost his cool. He was sick of Starr's resilience.

Not giving a damn that Starr was a female, Rich started wailing on her ass like she was a nigga in the street.

Starr's head rocked on her shoulders like a baseball bobble head as Rich brutally punched her in the face over and over again.

WHAP!

WHAP!

WHAP!

WHAP!

Starr's chair rocked a little, threatening to tip over but luckily it didn't. Rich was just about to punch Diamond again when Mama Keys suddenly made her way downstairs.

"That's enough," she said in a calm, yet authoritative voice.

Reluctantly, Rich ceased his brutal assault on Starr. He looked at his mother standing in the doorway, and was tempted to tell her that Starr was the reason behind her son's death...but he couldn't dare bring himself to do it.

"Don't you have some business you need to take care of?" Mama Keys asked, folding her arms across her chest.

Rich didn't respond immediately as he stared at his mother. "Yeah, I do," he finally answered. Without another word, he walked past his mother and headed upstairs.

Mama Keys shook her head as she slowly made her way over towards Starr. The poor girl was barely conscious and recognizable after the pummeling she'd taken.

"Please," Starr whispered. "Please...help...me..."

Mama Keys kneeled down in front of Starr. One of her eyes was swollen shut and her entire face was bruised and bloodied. Starr looked as if she'd just gotten out of the ring with Floyd Mayweather.
"Please...," Starr whispered. "Help me..."

Mama Keys looked at Starr with earnest eyes. "I'm sorry, baby. I don't get involved in my son's affairs," she said.

"Please...," Starr squeaked out. Her face throbbed in pain and she wished like hell that she was trapped in some sick, twisted nightmare. "Please help me..."

Mama Keys sighed in disappointment. "Don't beg sweetie...it's unbecoming," she said. "Let me tell you a lil' story." She reached for the bucket of warm water nearby. Inside was the same washcloth she'd used to clean Starr's face last night. "I had to have been in my early thirties," Mama Keys began, wringing out the washcloth. "I wasn't in the game too long—well, long enough to know what I was doing, but not long enough to know shit about the consequences I could face from my reckless actions." She gently wiped the blood of Starr's face. "I fucked up by playing with a connect's money..."

Mama Keys held up her left hand. She was missing two fingers. "I guess the moral of my story is 'for every mistake, there's a consequence'."

19

Gucci Mane and Trinidad James' *"Guwop"* blared through the massive speakers inside of Fantasy's Gentlemen's Club. As always it was rocking and going hard. The fellas were tossing cash in the air, and the hottest performers in Cleveland were doing their thing and representing for their establishment.

Rich sat at the bar sipping on a beer and shot of Hennessey. So much shit was on his mind that evening, primarily the unyielding female he had trapped inside of his mother's soundproof basement.

Why won't this bitch break, Rich thought to himself.

"Can I talk to you?"

Rich turned in the barstool and noticed Tatiana standing on his right hand side. Her arms were folded underneath her perky breasts and there was a no-nonsense expression on her pretty face.

Here we go.

"What's up, boo?" he asked, in a less than enthusiastic tone.

"Word on the street is you're back with that Diamond chick," Tatiana said with much attitude. "I just think that's fucked up. Shit, nigga, I've been holding you down—"

"Whoa! Whoa! Whoa!" Rich cut her off. He really didn't have time for her petty shit right now. "Tati, we been *fuckin'*," he corrected her. "Don't get it fucked up. You ain't did shit for me but toss me some pussy every now and then. And instead of bein' so preoccupied with keepin' yo' ear to the streets about what the fuck I'm doin', how 'bout you focus on the hustle. And then you wanna bitch and complain that you don't make as much as the other girls."

Tatiana rolled her eyes in response.

Rich then handed her a crisp fifty dollar bill. "Now get up out my face and give my mans over there a couple lap dances." He pointed towards a young dude sitting alone in the farthest corner of the club. Rich didn't even know who he was to be buying him complimentary dances, but he'd do anything to get Tatiana off his back.

Snatching the bill, Tatiana stomped off without another word.

Just when Rich thought he was in the clear, Cymphanie sauntered over towards him with drama written all over her face.

Her body looked incredible in a two piece purple rhinestone outfit and the black knee high stripper heels she wore only added to her sexiness.

Rich sighed in irritation. "All this money in here and ya'll bitches can't stay outta my face," he mumbled.

Cymphanie didn't hear his comment as she slid beside him. "Bay, this wasn't what I had in mind when I said I wanna come back," she told him.

"Yeah, but you back ain't you? You here—"

"I meant I wanted to be back with you," Cymphanie confessed. "I didn't wanna be right back where I started."

Rich took a swig from his beer. "Cymph, I gave ya ass ten grand so you could have a better life," he said. "Ya ass ain't did shit, but piss away my money. I even heard you gotta mothafuckin' son you don't even take care of—"

"What does my son have to do with this, Rich? Leave my son outta this—"

"I'ma tell you some shit my moms told me when I was a young nigga," Rich said. "She told me 'the instructions you follow, determines the future you create'."

Cymphanie frowned. "What the hell does that mean?" she asked.

Rich stood to his feet. "You think about it and figure it out. But until then I'ma need you to work back my ten grand." With that said he walked off, leaving Cymphanie to replay his wise words.

***

"Look, bitch, I don't know whatever type of game you on, but you're starting to piss me the hell off. I thought you loved me still. I thought you cared about me. But I guess now that you gotta 'nother person in yo' life you pretty much said fuck me. That's fucked up Starr, and you know it. If you needed me I'd be there for you without a doubt. I guess that's the difference between us, huh, hoe? And to think I actually missed you—I'm happy I did your dumb ass the way I did. You deserved every mothafuckin' thing you got—and guess what? Diamond ain't the only bitch I cheated on you with." Stevie chuckled. "There were others. Plenty others...sometimes I would even come home and kiss you in the mouth after I got done suckin' some pussy, and you were too stupid and blind to even notice. Fuck you Starr. I hope whatever dirty ass nigga you fuckin' with gives you AIDS—"

BEEP!

Starr's voicemail indicated that Stevie had used all of the allotted time. Riled up and disappointed at the same time, she disconnected the call. She'd everything she needed to say. It was unfortunate that Stevie had no clue that Starr was being against her will tied to a wooden chair in a basement.

***

Diamond was just about to do a line of coke on Rich's glass coffee table when the sudden knocking at the front door stopped her.

Sucking her teeth, she stood to her feet and made her way towards the front door. Rich was out and about and she was all alone in the luxurious mini mansion to do whatever she pleased.

When Diamond peered through the peephole she nearly fainted. Without hesitation, she swung the front door open and stood face to face with Stevie.

"Bitch, are you crazy?!" Diamond asked, both shocked and irritated by Stevie's presence. "You can't just be blowin' down. What if Rich was here?" She poked her head outside of the door and looked around at her surroundings. Diamond was paranoid about someone seeing Stevie.

"Girl, chill out," Stevie said, stepping around Diamond into Rich's lavish home. "I been outside waitin' for the nigga to scram," she said, taking in the décor of the elegant house. Stevie had never been inside of Rich's home.

Diamond's eyes widened in disbelief. "You were outside *waiting*?!" she repeated skeptically. She hoped her ears were deceiving her. "Hoe, you being a little reckless now, ain't you?" Diamond hurriedly closed the front door, but not before she scoped out the surroundings a final time.

"No, I'm *desperate*," Stevie corrected her. "A mothafucka sleepin' in her car and shit. I'm broke as hell. I ain't eatin'. I'm lookin' over my shoulder all the time. This ain't no way to live. Shit, I'm desperate as fuck."

Stevie then took off walking through Rich's home as if she owned the place.

Oh my goodness. She's gonna get us both fucked up, Diamond thought to herself.

"So did you start lookin' for the nigga's stash or have you been too busy fuckin' and getting' pampered?" Stevie asked in a sarcastic tone, not looking in Diamond's direction.

Diamond nervously followed Stevie through Rich's house. She wished Stevie would just leave. If Rich walked into his home at that very moment and saw Stevie, he'd kill the both of them without so much as a second thought.

"Stevie, I can't do this shit overnight," Diamond said. "I can handle it."

Stevie immediately stopped in her tracks at the sight of the cocaine lying temptingly on the coffee table.

"Oh, you can handle it, huh?" Stevie turned towards Diamond. "Bitch, how the fuck you gon' handle shit and you sittin' on yo' ass sniffing this garbage up ya nose?!"

Diamond opened her mouth, but closed it when she realized she didn't have anything to say.

Suddenly, Stevie charged Diamond and slammed her against the living room wall. The back of Diamond's head harshly smacked against it.

Stevie snatched Diamond up by the collar of her crop top. "Bitch, are you even in on this shit with me?! Cuz it looks like you gettin' a lil' too mothafuckin' comfortable."

"I'm in it with you, Stevie," Diamond assured her. "I was just waiting—stalling—that's all. I need a lil' time—"

"Bitch, time for what?!" Stevie yelled, saliva splattering Diamond's face.

Diamond slowly wiped the spit off her face. "Damn, bitch, you spitting on me and shit.

Just chill. I put Rich on to a coke connect and he re-up this Friday," she explained. "I'll follow his ass to the stash house. He won't even know it or suspect it. Me and you will murk his ass and take the work *and* the money. Simple as that."

A smile tugged at the corners of Stevie's heart shaped lips. She slowly loosened her grip on Diamond's shirt after hearing the foolproof plan. "Now that's what I'm talkin' 'bout," she said.

Diamond relaxed a little and fixed her shirt.

Stevie put some much needed space between them. "I knew you wouldn't let me down," Stevie told her.

"Did you ever get in contact with Starr?" Diamond asked.

Stevie sucked her teeth. "Man, she on some other shit. Fuck Starr."

20

The following morning Mama Keys tried her best to ignore the putrid odor of urine as she fed Starr a glass of ice cold water.

Starr greedily guzzled down the water considering she'd been stuck in a cold basement for two whole days with no food or nothing to drink. Water spilled down her chin as she quickly gulped down the refreshing liquid.

Starr looked and felt like shit. Her lips were dry and cracked. Her hair was in disarray, and she smelled like day old piss. Suddenly, Starr went in a brief coughing fit after drinking the water too rapidly.

"Easy. Easy now," Mama Keys told her.

After Starr finished with the glass of water, Mama Keys fed her a fresh blueberry muffin which she anxiously scarfed down. It relieved Starr's hunger pains, but she was still starving.

Mama Keys wiped away and all evidence that she'd just fed Starr. "Rich would flip if he knew I was down here feeding you," she told Starr.

Starr looked at Mama Keys through bruised and blackened eyes. "I'm pregnant...," she whispered.

"What?" Mama Keys asked, apparently not hearing her.

"I'm pregnant," Starr repeated in a louder tone. "I need to go to a hospital...or a clinic...anywhere but here in this basement..."

Mama Keys frowned and shook her head in disappointment. She obviously didn't believe Starr.

"I'm telling the truth," Starr stressed. "Please..."

Mama Keys folded her arms. "What did I tell you about begging?" she asked. "It's unbecoming—"

"You have to believe me!" Starr cried. "Please believe me—I can prove it to you!"

Mama Keys' expression turned from disappointment into sympathy. If Starr was in fact pregnant then there was no way she could sit back and condone that kind of violence or torture in her home.

"Please...just go get a test from the drug store. I can prove to you that I'm pregnant...Please..."

Mama Keys unfolded her arms and allowed them to drop loosely at her sides.

For a moment, Starr thought she might actually hit her out of anger that she might be being lied to. Of course, the strike never came.

Slowly, Mama Keys backed away from Starr. Without another word, she made her way upstairs, leaving Starr alone to wonder if she believed her or not.

***

Rich rolled over and positioned himself between Diamond's thick thighs.

There was no kind of sex better than morning sex.

Diamond gasped as he pushed his entire nine inches inside her warm, gushy pussy. "Shit," she moaned. "Not too deep baby."

Rich nibbled on her bottom lip. "You better take this dick how I give it to you." He slipped his tongue inside her mouth and kissed her passionately. "This pussy shouldn't be so damn deep."

Diamond rotated her hips underneath him, matching his slow even strokes with her own. "Why'd you let me come back?" she whispered, gazing into his eyes.

Rich pinned Diamond's hands above her head, and with his free hand squeezed on a breast. "You know why…"

Diamond sucked on his bottom lip. "I want you to tell me."

After a brief kissing session Rich finally answered her question. "Even though you ain't good for me…you're good *to* me. You compliment a nigga," he said. "You might even fuck around and play me again…but that's a risk I'm willing to take."

***

Starr's heart beat rapidly in her chest as she listened to the heavy footsteps making their way down the flight of steps. Initially, she feared it might be Rich returning to work her over some more.

The moment Starr saw Mama Keys she breathed a sigh of relief—until she noticed the sharp knife clutched tightly in her right hand.

Starr immediately tensed up. "Please! No!" she cried in fear.

Mama Keys ignored Starr's pleas as she bent down and cut the tape off her legs. Afterward she freed Starr's hands.

Starr was both surprised and confused as she sat rubbing her sore wrists. Red marks from the duct tape were imprinted in her light skin.

Mama Keys reached in her back pocket and pulled out a single pregnancy test strip. "There's a bathroom right over there," she said, pointing to the small room located near the washer and dryer.

Starr slowly took the pregnancy test from her, but Mama Keys didn't let go of it immediately.

"If you're lying to me, I'll kill you myself," she threatened before releasing the pregnancy test.

Starr looked down at the knife in Mama Keys hand and swallowed the large lump that had formed in her throat. An uncomfortable feeling settled in the pit of her stomach.

"Yes ma'am," Starr muttered before slowly making her way towards the basement's bathroom.

Mama Keys patiently waited outside of the door for Starr to handle her business. Rich would've had a fucking fit if he knew his beloved mother had untied Starr, especially since he had so many horrible things in store for her.

Inside the bathroom, Starr's nerves were on edge. She'd never been so distressed and fearful in her entire life.

Sometimes these things aren't even accurate, Starr thought to herself. *What if it comes back negative?*

She was nervous when she squatted over the test strip that her stream of urine accidentally splashed onto her hand.

Twenty seconds felt like an eternity as Starr patiently waited for the outcome of the test results. With trembling fingers, she lifted the pregnancy test strip to read...

21

Rich gently pushed Diamond's left leg back so that her toes were touching the headboard. He plunged in deeper and then slid out halfway before diving back in.

"*Oooohh*! Damn, baby!" Diamond whimpered. Her toes curled as Rich stroked her insides until she came for the third time that morning.

BOOM!

BOOM!

BOOM!

The sudden knocking at the front door was followed by the doorbell ringing incessantly.

"Who's that?" Diamond asked.

"Hell, I don't know. Let me go see—"

"No. No. No. No. Don't stop!" Diamond pleaded. She grabbed onto his ass in order to hold him in place. "I was just about to cum again."

"I gotta see who it is, bay. It might be business," Rich told her, climbing out the bed.

Diamond pouted as she watched him pull on a robe and leave the bedroom.

Rich padded barefoot to the large solid, wooden front door. Without looking through the peephole first, he swung the front door open.

"What the hell...? What are you doin' here?" Rich asked both surprised and confused.

Standing on his doorstep as if she'd been invited was Cymphanie with her suitcases beside her and a wide grin on her beautiful face.

***

Starr sat in the passenger seat of Mama Keys' 2012 Mercedes e350. There was an unbearable amount of tension in the vehicle as they sat parked right outside of the clinic.

"I'ma tell you right now before we even get in here, don't try any funny shit," Mama Keys warned Starr. "Because my son *will* find you...and my son *will* kill you..."

Starr didn't like the sound of that threat, and she didn't doubt it in the least.

"I understand," Starr mumbled. She felt as if she were being scolded by a no-nonsense parent instead of the mother of her kidnapper.

In all actuality, Starr did contemplate running inside and demanding for someone to notify the police. However, now that Mama Keys had put that threat in her head she doubted she'd be trying any slick shit.

"I hope I'm making myself clear," Mama Keys said with a serious expression.

Starr studied the wrinkles in Mama Keys' forehead and the coldness in her large eyes. She wasn't fucking around and she wanted Starr to know just that.

Not waiting for a reply, Mama Keys' opened the door and stepped out. Starr quickly followed suit.

This is not how I imagined things to go, Starr thought to herself.

She'd expected her baby's father to accompany her to her first doctor's visit.

***

Diamond walked up out of nowhere and gave Cymphanie a suspicious look. She was pissed that her sex session had been interrupted by some bitch.

"Bay, who is this?" Diamond asked with a disgusted look on her face.

Cymphanie was obviously dressed to impress Rich in her black leather and mesh bodysuit. Large gold discs hung from her lobes and her short hair was still wet from the shower she'd taken not too long ago.

"No, bitch, who are *you*?!" Cymphanie looked her up and down. She was pissed at the sight of Diamond wearing one of Rich's t-shirts. She felt that she should be wearing it and walking around his house as if she owned it. After all, she was once his main chick.

"*Bitch*?!" Diamond asked, clearly offended.

She walked up on Cymphanie preparing to give her the business, but Rich quickly jumped in between both women. This wasn't the first time he had to referee a fight over him between two women. However, right now he wasn't in the mood for the extra shit. In a couple hours, he had to pick up the work from LaVelle and hit up his stash house.

"Look, chill ya'll. Cymph, it ain't even that type of party no mo'. You had yo' chance, ma," he shrugged nonchalantly.

Both Cymphanie's pride and feelings were hurt.

"You heard him. Buh-bye," Diamond teased, waving her fingers for good measure.

"*Bitch*!" Cymphanie screamed, charging at Diamond.

Before Diamond could even think to defend herself, Cymphanie ran up and slapped the shit out of her. Diamond had no idea that she was fighting Starr's cousin when the two women broke out into a full-on brawl inside of Rich's foyer.

Diamond slammed Cymphanie against the nearby wooden accent table and accidentally knocked over the vase and decoratives.

"Aye, chill! Chill! Chill!" Rich barked, breaking the two women up.

This also wasn't his first time breaking up a fight between two women over him.

"Bitch, you better hope I don't see you on the street!" Diamond threatened.

"Hoe, I'ma dogwalk yo' ass the next time I see you!" Cymphanie promised. She was now missing an earring.

"Come on, Cymph. You gotta bounce," Rich said, pulling her towards the door. "Comin' over here startin' shit, I ain't got time for this."

Cymphanie snatched away from him and stormed out the front door. "Fuck you, nigga!" she yelled. "And what the fuck you do to my cousin?! Ever since I gave you her address she ain't been answerin' her mothafuckin' phone!"

Rich stepped outside barefoot and closed the door behind himself so that Diamond couldn't hear their conversation.

"Don't worry about what the fuck I do—"

"Oh, I ain't worried about it—but the police will be when I report a kidnap—"

Cymphanie didn't get a chance to finish her sentence before Rich's large hand was wrapped around her throat.

"You know what, bitch? You talk too mothafuckin' much?" he spat. "That's yo' problem. That's always been yo' damn problem. And you ain't slick, bitch," Rich told her. "I know all about ya lil' scams on these niggas you been doin'. Got almost every hood nigga in Columbus lookin' for yo' ass. Maybe I should do 'em all a favor and handle yo' ass right here and right now."

Cymphanie's face puffed up and her eyes became watery as Rich brutally crushed her windpipes. She just knew he was about to kill her for talking recklessly.

So this is how it ends, she thought to herself. *He's going to be the one to take me out?*

Rich's grip around her throat tightened. He looked her dead in the eyes. Cymphanie had never seen him look so angry or deranged, and she was sad that this would be the final thing she saw before she died. She always imagined she'd die peacefully...not violent...not like this.

Seconds before Cymphanie succumbed to unconsciousness Rich released her throat and tossed her onto the ground as if she were a rag doll.

The thin leather material ripped after she crashed onto the concrete.

"Bitch, get the fuck off my property before I change my mind about killin' ya ass," Rich said.

Cymphanie didn't have to be told twice as she scurried to her feet and ran frantically to her BMW parked in the driveway.

"Fuck you, Rich!" she yelled, now that her hand was on the doorknob of her car. "You ain't shit, nigga! I can't believe I came back here for you!"

"Quit tryin' to run the streets and take care of yo' mothafuckin' kid!"

"I hope you burn in hell you heartless mothafucka!" Cymphanie screamed before hopping inside her car and peeling off.

22

"Congratulations, Ms. Coleman, it looks like you're eleven weeks pregnant—"

"Eleven weeks?!" Starr repeated in disbelief. "But—I—how...I hardly had any symptoms."

Starr's doctor offered a reassuring smile. "And that's perfectly normal for a first-time pregnancy. Maybe your body just didn't want you to know yet." She then looked up at Mama Keys and grinned. "Congratulations."

Starr was in a world of her own as she stared off into space. *So it is Antoine's baby*, she said to herself. *Where do I go from here?*

Starr's doctor handed her a few ultrasound pictures, and Starr anxiously looked them over. "When will I know what I'm having?" she asked.

"Usually around twenty or so weeks," the doctor explained. Her expression then turned into that of a serious one. "Just so you know, the clinic does offer counseling....," she said surveying Starr's bruised and battered face.

"There won't be any need for that," Mama Keys cut in.

***

Mama Keys and Starr sat silently inside of the Mercedes after the news. The moment should have been a proud and exciting one, but Starr had no idea what her fate would be. She was pregnant with Antoine's baby and she hadn't spent any real time with him other than the quickie in the gas station. There was also the very big issue with Rich. Starr knew that even if his mother did tell him that she was pregnant he wouldn't give a fuck. It wasn't like the kid was his and Rich already proved to be a heartless, cynical motherfucker. He'd probably end up letting his homeboys rape Starr to the point she miscarried.

Starr shuddered at the very thought. She then pushed the disturbing image to the back of her mind and lightly touched her stomach.

I can't believe a baby is growing inside of me.

Her stomach felt hard to the touch but she welcomed the different, new feel.

I can't believe it.

Suddenly, Mama Keys broke the nerve-wracking silence by speaking up. "Leave," she said. "Don't look back. I'll deal with Rich."

Starr couldn't believe her ears. She slowly turned to face Rich's mother.

"I'm giving you a second chance...and that's something I rarely—if ever—do."

For several seconds, Starr stared at Mama Keys in silence. Words couldn't express how grateful she was considering she was the cause of her son's death. Unbeknownst to Starr, Mama Keys had no idea that Starr had helped kill Cartier...because if she did she would've killed the young girl herself.

Fortunately, fate was on Starr's side.

"Thank you," Starr whispered. She then opened the door and climbed out before Mama Keys could change her mind.

***

Rich jogged down the steps of his mother's basement expecting to see Starr tied to a wooden chair—but was instead met with the unexpected sight of an empty seat and cut up duct tape on the floor.

"The fuck?"

"She's gone," Mama Keys said, slowly making her way down the stairs. "I let her go." Her voice was strong and authoritative and she dared him, or anyone else for that matter, to go against whatever she said. "That damn girl was pregnant. I didn't want that shit on my conscious," Mama Keys explained. "I need to be able to sleep peacefully at night."

It was then that Rich felt a little bad about manhandling Starr the way he did now that he knew she was pregnant. However, he quickly shook the feeling off when he remembered how she had helped kill his little brother. Rich thought about spazzing out on his mother for letting Starr go, but then he remembered that he wouldn't even need her anyway after tonight.

"It's all good," Rich said. "She was useless anyway." He'd finally gotten word on Stevie's whereabouts, and now it was time to dish out some much-deserved revenge.

23

The sun was just beginning to set as Diamond kept a safe distance behind Rich's silver 2011 Acura TL. He was driving low-key tonight so that he wouldn't draw too much attention to himself as he made his way to his stash point.

Pulling out her cellphone, Diamond dialed Stevie's number.

She picked up on the second ring. "What's up?" she answered, hype and anxious to give Rich's ass the business.

"Aight, I'm following him now," Diamond told her. "I'll call you after it's done—"

"Diamond, you sure you don't want me there with you? What if—"

"I can handle it on my own," Diamond argued. "He won't even see the shit coming. Besides, he's alone."

Stevie paused and thought about it. "You sure?" she asked.

"He trusts me," Diamond told her. "He won't even see the shit coming. I promise you. I'll call you with the directions on how to get there as soon as it's done."

"Aight. Be careful."

Diamond disconnected the phone call and continued following closely behind Rich.

Time to show and prove.

***

Knock!

Knock!

Knock!

Knock!

Cymphanie waited patiently outside of Jason's, her baby father, house. Suddenly, she remembered that she was missing an earring and quickly took out the other one before anyone came to the door. The last thing Cymphanie wanted was for Jason's girlfriend to answer the door and see her half-stepping as far as her looks.

Cymphanie raised her fist to knock on the door again, but stopped when she heard the sound of the door being unlocked.

Jason swung the front door open wearing nothing but a pair of gray sweatpants and an irritated expression on his handsome face.

Cymphanie's mouth watered at the sight of his toned physique. She'd actually forgotten just how sexy the father of her child was, and for a moment she tried to remember why she had even left him in the first place.

"What are you doing here?" Jason asked, snapping Cymphanie from her provocative thoughts.

It was then that Cymphanie replayed Rich's words over in her mind.

The instructions you follow, determines the future you create.

"I'm here because I'd like to start being a part of my son's life," Cymphanie said.

Jason was shocked out of his mind to hear those words. For a moment, he wondered if his baby mother was drunk or high. Since the day she had pushed their son out, Cymphanie had treated him as if he didn't exist. She would much rather run the streets than face the responsibility of being someone's parent.

"Excuse me?" Jason asked. "Am I hearin' you correctly? I ain't trippin' am I?"

"No," Cymphanie answered. "You're not trippin'."

Jason leaned against the doorway and stared suspiciously at Cymphanie as if he were trying to read her. "Wow...what's gotten into you today?"

Common sense.

"Where's your girl?" Cymphanie asked, looking over Jason's shoulder.

Jason snorted. "What girl?" he asked. "Thanks to you and the bomb you dropped at the mall, she dipped on my ass."

Cymphanie faked disappointment and sympathy. "I'm sorry about that," she said in her sweetest tone. However, the truth of the matter was she hated Jamie and was glad that the stuck up bitch was finally out of the picture. "Is it cool if I come inside?" she asked.

Jason stepped to the side and allowed Cymphanie entrance.

***

Stevie answered her cellphone the moment it rang. "Tell me something good," Stevie told Diamond, anxious to make her move.

"It's done," Diamond simply said.

"You did it?" Stevie asked in disbelief.

"I killed him," Diamond clarified.

"Wh—How?" Stevie asked, shocked by Diamond's brazenness.

"Damn, bitch. You wanna play by play on how I killed Rich? I shot his ass in the back of his head. Point blank. Now hurry up and get your ass down here and help me get this money and work."

24

Stevie met Diamond at Rich's stash point which was nothing more than a dilapidated abandoned church on the outskirts of town.

Pulling her car alongside Rich's, Stevie didn't have a doubt in her mind that Diamond had actually gone through with killing Rich. She always thought she'd be the one that would take his ass out like she did Cartier, but Stevie wasn't complaining about someone else handling her dirty work.

She only wished she was there to witness Rich get his brains blown out. He was always walking around like he was a king or some shit, but after tonight his entire empire would fall thanks to Stevie and Diamond's plan.

Stevie took a quick pull on the Black and Mild and then put it out in the ashtray. Her heart pounded rapidly in her chest as she experienced both nervousness and excitement. Pulling herself together, she slowly exited her vehicle and made her way inside the demolished church building.

Rubble crunched underneath her Timberland boots as she entered the church. It was partially lit by a single lamp placed on top of the podium.

"Diamond?" Stevie called out, looking around at her surroundings. Just being there gave her goose bumps.

"I'm right here!" Diamond yelled back.

Stevie then noticed Diamond standing several feet from where she stood near the ran down church pew. A black duffel bag hung loosely off her shoulder.

"Where is he?" Stevie asked, making her way over towards Diamond. She tried her best to step around debris as she navigated towards her. "Where's Rich's body? I wanna see the nigga's body before we bounce," she insisted.

"I'm right here," Rich said, seemingly appearing out of nowhere.

Immediately, Stevie whirled around after hearing his voice behind her.

POP!

"*Aaahh!*" Stevie cried out. She instantly hit the ground and grabbed her wounded leg. It took her brain several seconds to register that Diamond had just shot her. "You mothafuckin' bitch! You set me up!"

Blood gushed from the bullet wound in her calf muscle. She'd never experienced so much pain in her life...but nothing hurt worse than the betrayal that she was experiencing at that very moment.

"You set yourself up," Diamond said unsympathetically.

Rich chuckled and shook his head at Stevie's stupidity as he made his way over towards Diamond. "I been waitin' for this mothafuckin' moment," he said.

"Fuck ya'll!" Stevie spat. "Fuck both of ya'll asses!"

Rich gradually took the Glock from Diamond.

"See daddy. I told you I would show you the type of female I am."

Rich smiled, pulled Diamond close and snaked his tongue inside her mouth. After the passionate kiss, he turned towards Stevie lying pathetically on the ground.

She tried to scoot away from him, but with an injured leg she didn't get too far. "If I could, I'd kill that nigga Cartier a thousand times over!" Stevie laughed sadistically. "He was a bitch ass power hungry mothafucka! Just like you!" she spat. "I hope his punk ass burnin' in hell!"

Rich aimed the gun towards Stevie's head. "Well then, give the nigga my regards..."

POP!

A single bullet tore through Stevie's head before exiting the back of her skull.

***

The following afternoon Starr made her way towards the entrance of the gas store Antoine was employed at. Butterflies fluttered in her tummy, and she hadn't rehearsed a single line of what she'd say to him.

Ding-Ding!

The bell above the door chimed indicating Starr's entrance. The moment she stepped inside her eyes wandered over towards the cash register. Antoine was busy ringing up a customer and initially didn't notice her standing there.

After ringing and bagging up the customer's items, Antoine's gaze slowly wandered over towards Starr.

She waited patiently to see what his reaction would be.

A slowly smile spread across his lips.

Starr breathed a sigh of relief and immediately smiled afterward.

THE END

CPSIA information can be obtained
at www.ICGtesting.com
Printed in the USA
LVOW11s2221270217
525565LV00001B/61/P